His name is Evan Michael Tanner. He is thirty-four years old and he hasn't slept a wink since a piece of shrapnel destroyed the sleep center in his brain during the Korean War.

Tanner loves lost causes and beautiful women. The FBI has a thick file on him; the CIA taps his phone. And a super-secret intelligence agency wants him to be their man.

But Tanner is his own man. And to prove it he's willing to smuggle fifteen people out of Russia—even if it means bringing the world to the brink of global war...

_____

*"Block generates nonstop suspense."*

—PUBLISHERS WEEKLY

# LAWRENCE BLOCK

# TANNER'S TWELVE SWINGERS

A JOVE BOOK

This Jove book contains the complete
text of the original edition.
It has been completely reset in a typeface
designed for easy reading, and was printed
from new film.

TANNER'S TWELVE SWINGERS

A Jove Book/published by arrangement with
the author

PRINTING HISTORY
Fawcett Publications edition published 1967
Jove edition/February 1985

ISBN: 0-515-08106-X

Jove books are published by The Berkley Publishing Group,
200 Madison Avenue, New York, N.Y. 10016.
The words "A JOVE BOOK" and the "J" with sunburst
are trademarks belonging to Jove Publications, Inc.
PRINTED IN THE UNITED STATES OF AMERICA

# 1

---

On my third day in Athens I sat at a small square table at the airport cafe watching a sleek Air India jet taxi down the runway, rise abruptly into the air, then break cloud cover and disappear from view. One of the seventy-nine passengers bound for London carried a passport that identified him as Evan Michael Tanner, American.

The passport lied. I am Evan Michael Tanner, American, and it was with mixed emotions that I watched my passport wing its way out of my life.

Across the table from me, Georgios Melas raised his glass in a silent toast to the departing plane. I lifted my own and sipped ouzo. It tasted like licorice whips on the tongue, like fire in the chest.

"You are unhappy," Georgios said.

"Not entirely."

1

"And on such a magnificent day!"

"A cloudy day."

"A few clouds——"

"It's getting cold. I think it's going to rain."

"Ah, and you worry about Pindaris on the plane. It will land safely in London, do not worry. And Pindaris will be safe in London."

It would have been unworthy to admit that I was worried about Pindaris chiefly in his capacity as custodian of my passport. Pindaris was an intense young Greek from the island of Andros who had recently revealed his discontent with the Greek government by hurling a cannister bomb at a car that then contained the Minister of Defense. The bomb had not gone off. The alarm had, however, and Pindaris was hotter than Death Valley at high noon.

Since Pindaris was a fellow member of the Pan-Hellenic Friendship Society and since his English was good enough to convince an Englishman that he was an American, it had seemed only proper that I turn my passport over to him. He in turn had sworn on his mother's grave that he would have the passport returned to my apartment in New York.

"It will be home before you are," he had said more than once. And I could well believe it.

I sipped more ouzo, comforting myself with the thought that the passport would have been of little use to me for the near future. Once I crossed the Yugoslav border, a passport with my name on it would become a distinct liability. It would only serve to identify me to the Yugoslav authorities, who would respond by hanging me. I had once started a revolution in Yugoslavia, and such activity is apt to render one *persona non grata* almost anywhere.

Georgios motioned for more ouzo. "It is a noble thing you have done, Evan," he said solemnly. "The Pan-Hellenic

2

Friendship Society will not be quick to forget this."

"To the Society," I said, and we drank again. But for the Pan-Hellenic Friendship Society, my passport would not have been en route to London at that very moment. But for the Latvian Army-In-Exile, I would not have been on my way to Latvia. But for the Internal Macedonian Revolutionary Organization, I would not have been preparing to slip across the Yugoslav frontier at the first opportunity.

And yet, I had to admit, all of this was not entirely true. As it happened, I was on my way to Latvia because I did not want to go to Colombia and because Karlis Mielovicius was my friend. Karlis was also a Lett, and Letts are incurable romantics, and Karlis was a Lett with his home in Providence, Rhode Island, and his heart in Riga, Latvia.

That's why I was going to Latvia.

I was going by way of Macedonia not because it was the shortest way to Latvia or the safest way to Latvia or the most sensible way to Latvia.

I was going to Macedonia to see my son.

In Georgios' house on the outskirts of Athens he and I drank still more ouzo while his wife stuffed tender vine leaves with rice and pine nuts and minced lamb. After dinner we switched to coffee. It was raining outside, as I had thought it might. We warmed ourselves in front of the wood fire, and I opened my flat leather satchel and took out a small charcoal sketch.

It showed a baby, and the baby looked like a baby. Cameras are scarce in Macedonia, and artists there have not been forced into abstraction by the advance of technology. Their task, as they see it, is to convey as well as possible the exact appearance of whatever it is they are drawing. This particular unknown artist had been drawing a baby,

3

and that's exactly what the sketch looked like.

"A beautiful baby," I said aloud.

Georgios and his wife examined the sketch and agreed with my estimation. "He resembles you," Zoe Melas said. "About the eyes and I think the mouth as well."

"He's plump like his mother."

"He is in New York?"

"He is in Macedonia."

"Ah," she said. "And you go to see him?"

"Tonight."

"Tonight!" She darted a look of alarm at Georgios, then fastened her gaze upon me. "But it is a long journey," she said, "and you have been awake since early this morning. You were sitting before the fire when I myself arose. You could not have had much sleep last night."

I had not had any sleep the past night. Nor, indeed, had I had any sleep in the past seventeen years, ever since a piece of North Korean shrapnel found its way into my skull and destroyed something called the sleep center, all of which was a source of considerable confusion to the army physicians, who wondered why the hell I seemed to be awake twenty-four hours a day, day after blessed day. Since the phenomenon confuses ordinary mortals as well as doctors, I didn't bother explaining it to Zoe and Georgios. I said only that I was not at all tired and that I wanted to get to Macedonia as soon as possible.

"I might arrange for a car," Georgios said.

"I would appreciate it."

"The Society has many friends. One could obtain a car and drive you north toward the border. But as for crossing the border——"

"I can manage that."

"The frontier is fortified."

"I know."

4

"You have crossed before?"

I nodded. I had crossed from Yugoslavia into Greece a few months before my son was born and on that occasion I was escorting a Slovak Nazi in a cataleptic coma. Tonight's trip figured to be comparatively simple.

"You will want warm clothes," Georgios said. "Perhaps you would be better off wearing the clothing of a peasant."

"Yes."

"And you will need food," Zoe said. "I will pack food for you. Meat and cheese and bread."

"That would be good."

"And brandy," Georgios said.

I was on my way well before midnight. I wore thick-soled shoes and heavy overalls and a worn leather jacket with several sweaters beneath it. Between two of these sweaters I had tucked my leather satchel. On my lap I had a small cloth sack that Zoe had packed with food and in my pocket I had a flat pint bottle that Georgios had filled with Metaxa brandy.

My driver was a silent, thick-bodied Greek whose main interest lay in testing the legendary durability of his little Volkswagen. The roads north of Athens were a far cry from turnpikes, but he bounced the car over ruts and spun it around curves with the resolution of one who is convinced of his own immortality. In Thessalia our road wound its way through some fairly impressive mountains, with tortuous curves and sheer drops on either side. I tried not to look out the window. When this proved difficult, I sat back in my seat and numbed myself with little nips from the bottle of brandy.

By the time dawn was breaking, the Volkswagen had gone as far as my driver intended it should go. He stopped at a farmhouse a few miles from Velvendos in the Greek

5

sector of Macedonia. The farmer was a comrade who would give him food and a place to sleep until he was ready for the trip back to Athens. I shared the last of the bottle with him, and we drank deeply to the glory that was and would again be Greece. We shook hands warmly. He hurried off to the shelter of the farmhouse, and I walked through a gray and drizzling dawn toward the Yugoslav frontier.

I spent a few hours walking and slipping into character. For three days I had been speaking and thinking in Greek and now I had to shift mental gears and switch to the strain of Bulgarian spoken in Macedonia. I have been fluent in the language for several years, and it was only a question of making the proper mental adjustment. Languages have always come easily to me, and the more languages a person knows, the easier it is to add another to the string. All it takes is time.

And time is one commodity of which I am rarely in short supply. My endless insomnia has meant rather more to me than the $112 a month partial disability payment the Army graciously pays me. It has meant that I have at my disposal a full twenty-four hours a day, not the usual sixteen or so. Such an abundance of waking hours permits one to learn any number of languages and embrace any number of lost causes.

Here too a mental adjustment was required. I had spent time with Greek members of the Pan-Hellenic Friendship Society and was now heading toward members of the Internal Macedonian Revolutionary Organization. The Pan-Hellenists dreamed of a restoration of the old Greek empire, while the IMRO comrades pledged their lives to the vision of a Macedonia free and independent, independent not only of Yugoslavia but of Greece as well. My Pan-Hellenist brothers and my IMRO brothers would have cheerfully slit one another's throats.

6

By midmorning the rain had let up entirely. I practiced my Bulgarian on a succession of peasants who carried me a few miles each in donkey carts. I flashed IMRO signs at each of them. One or two seemed to recognize the signs but chose to ignore them, but ultimately a bull-necked goatherd with a thick brown moustache offered the appropriate countersign, and I gave him an abbreviated version of who I was and where I wanted to go.

"Evan Tanner," he said. "Who made the revolution in Tetovo."

"Yes."

"Todor Prolov will rejoice in your arrival."

"Todor died in the revolution. When the Serb troops crushed the revolutionary spirit of the people of Tetovo, Todor was killed."

"But his sister Mischa lives——"

"His sister is Annalya."

"Ah. As I have never seen you before, a test was in order. You bear me no resentment?"

"I am not the sort to resent caution."

He took a wedge of cheese from a sack in the back of his cart and cut sections for each of us. We washed down the cheese with resinous wine. He wiped his mouth with the back of his hand and asked in a whisper if I planned to start another rebellion.

"It is not time," I said.

"I agree. We must gather our forces. One may be impatient for open revolution, but in the meantime we put thorns in the side of the Belgrade dictatorship. An act of sabotage, an assassination—it is better to provoke, to sting like a hornet, for the time being. You agree?"

"I do."

"And you go where? To Tetovo?"

"Yes."

7

"For a special purpose?"

"To see my son," I said. I dug out the sketch and unfolded it. "My son," I said.

He studied it, nodded. "A good likeness."

"You've seen him?"

"Who has not? It is said that one day he will lead Macedonia." He looked at the sketch, then at me. "A strong resemblance. But Annalya and the boy no longer live in Tetovo. The authorities . . . it would be unsafe. They are in a village not far from Kavadar. You know where that is?"

"More or less."

"I will take you there."

"Can you get me across the border?"

"The border?" He began to laugh. "The *border?*" He made fists of his hands and pounded them against his meaty thighs. "The border? Because Greeks and Serbs draw an imaginary line across the heartland of Macedonia, does this mean that there is a border? Because despots and oppressors string barbed wire and post sentries, does this constitute a border?" He shook with laughter. "This border," he roared, "should not concern you."

The border obviously did not concern the goatherd. His first impulse was to round up a crew of comrades and raid a border post, killing a few sentries and opening up a hole in the border wide enough to march an army through. It was such acts of provocation, he explained, that kept nationalist spirit keen. I managed to talk him out of it, arguing that such a stir would make it more difficult for me once inside Yugoslavia. He agreed reluctantly.

"So we will find a place where the crossing may be managed with ease," he said. "We will be no more than a pair of stupid goatherds with our flock. Does a goat know of borders and barbed wire? A goat knows only that he must graze where he may. And once across the border, we shall

**8**

turn the goats over to a friend, and I shall lead you to where Annalya lives." His broad face split in a smile.

"By nightfall," he said, "you will be holding your son upon your knee."

# 2

----------------------------------------------------------------

By nightfall I was holding my son upon my knee.

And what a grand son he was! The sketch, however accurate in details and dimensions, had not done him justice at all. Charcoal could not capture the sweet animation of him, the sparkle of his dark eyes, the glow of his pink skin, the way his little hand curled around my finger with such strength and determination. The way he kicked and cried, the way he yawned in slow motion, the way he sucked methodically upon his thumb. The way he giggled foolishly when I, like a fool, made idiot faces at him.

"He is a healthy baby," Annalya said. "And very strong."

"How old is he?"

"Almost six months."

"He looks big."

"He is big for his age. And so fat."

Little Todor giggled at me again. His dark eyes focused

upon a spot a few feet in back of my head, then gradually zoomed in until he was staring intently at my nose.

"He likes me," I said.

"Of course. You are surprised?"

"I think he recognizes me."

"But of course he knows you. You are his father."

"He's a wise child," I said.

We sat cross-legged on the earthen floor of a little one-room hut a few miles outside of Kavadar. Annalya and Todor shared the hut with a childless peasant couple. The old woman had cooked supper for us, and then she and her husband had slipped out of the house to spend a few days with relatives a mile or two down the road. A few thick logs smoked on the hearth. The fire cast a shallow glow over my son and his mother.

Motherhood seemed to agree with Annalya. Her long blonde hair shone in the firelight. She leaned forward suddenly to wipe the corners of little Todor's mouth, and my eyes took in the rich curves of her full body, the full breasts bobbing braless beneath her heavy sweater, the lines of hip and thigh. I remembered the feel of that fine body beneath me on the night of young Todor's conception.

"Todor Tanirov," I said solemnly.

"You approve of his name?"

"Completely. He is named for a hero."

"He is named for two heroes," she said, and touched my arm. "But I will have to keep his patronym a secret when the boy goes to school. If the authorities knew his parentage, there would be trouble." She sighed. "But when he is of age and when he rallies the people of Macedonia to his side, then he shall call himself Todor Tanirov."

The subject of all this speculation began fussing. I picked him up, held him over my shoulder, patted him dutifully

12

upon the back. Instead of burping, he cried all the louder.

"A conspirator," I said, "should cry in whispers."

"He is hungry. Let me have him."

I handed over the crying infant, and she opened her sweater and presented him with a breast. It was immediately evident that this was precisely what the lad had in mind. His little mouth fastened upon the nipple, his hands positioned themselves on either side, and he nursed greedily.

"A hungry baby, Evan."

"He's his father's son. He knows what good is."

"Ah."

"Have you received the money I sent?"

"Yes. It was too much. I gave the excess to the IMRO."

"You should have kept it. For the boy."

"I kept enough for him." Todor lost the breast, and she guided his head back to it. "I was so happy that you remembered him, that you cared for him. I did not dare to dream that you would be able to come to Macedonia to see him with your eyes."

"I wish I could have come sooner."

"It is good that you waited. He was so red and shriveled when he was first born! You would not have liked him."

"I'd have loved him anyway."

I went to the fire and used a branch to push the smoking logs closer together. I sat down again at Annalya's side. She switched Todor form one breast to the other. He fussed at first, but then his hungry little mouth found what it wanted, and he devoted himself wholeheartedly to the business of feeding. I watched his eyes. They would fall slowly shut, then snap open, then drift shut again, but through it all he kept on eating ravenously.

When he had finally finished, she carried him to the little straw mattress at the left-hand side of the hearth. She set him down gently and covered him with a pair of knitted blankets. He did not open his eyes. She returned to my side and sat close to me.

"He is a good baby," she said. "He will sleep for hours."

"He sleeps well?"

"Like a young lamb."

"I'm glad to hear that," I said. Of course it could hardly have been otherwise; Lamarckian genetics and the inheritance of acquired characteristics has been rather thoroughly discredited, and even Lamarck would have hesitated to suggest that my shrapnel-induced insomnia would be passed on to my children. Still, it was reassuring to know that chance had not visited this particular malady upon little Todor. That sort of idiosyncrasy could be more readily coped with by a Manhattan-based ghost-writer than by a Macedonian peasant and revolutionary leader.

"Evan? Will you be here long?"

"A few days and nights."

"And then you return to America?"

I shook my head. "Not at once. I have business to the north."

"In Belgrade?"

"Farther than that."

"I wish you could stay longer, Evan."

I stretched out on the dirt floor. She lay down beside me. Her sweater buttoned down the front. The buttons were made of dark brown leather. I opened them one by one and put my hands on her breasts.

"See what the little one has done to them? They are empty now."

"They are magnificent, my love. My little bird."

"Ahh . . ."

We lay side by side on the floor with our arms around

**14**

one another. Her mouth tasted sweet and warm. My hands played merrily upon her lush breasts, and she giggled and told me that she knew now why Todor was such a fine nursing baby. "He takes after his father."

"I told you as much."

"Ah, Evan..."

Lazily, pausing for kisses and caresses, we removed our clothes in the flickering firelight. Childbirth had not harmed her body in the least. I touched the shallow bowl of her belly, the rich, sloping thighs.

"You have other women?"

"Some."

"And other children?"

"No."

"Todor is the only one?"

"Yes."

She sighed, contented. We kissed and clung to each other. We parted, and she drew me over to her own straw mattress on the other side of the hearth from Todor's.

"Todor will need brothers," she said.

"That is true."

"And it has been half a year since his birth. It is time."

"Yes. But what if we produce a girl?"

"A daughter?" She considered this while I handled her fine body. "But it is good for a boy to have sisters. And you will return again, Evan, so that there will be a time for more sons."

"For Macedonia."

"For Macedonia," she agreed. "And for me."

And I touched her some more, and we kissed, and she ran out of words as I ran out of thoughts. Her thighs parted in welcome, and her arms and legs gripped me fiercely, and the rude straw mattress groaned beneath our passion. I forgot

**15**

about the Letts and the Colombians and the pudgy man from Washington. I even forgot my sleeping son, for once I cried out in passion, and Annalya gripped me tight.

"Hush," she whispered. "You will wake Todor."

But the little angel went right on sleeping.

Later, a long while later, I put a few more logs on the fire. Annalya rounded up a jug of honey wine, and we sat in front of the fire sipping it. It was too sweet to drink very much of, but in small sips it went down nicely and helped the fire warm us.

"In a few days you must leave," she said.

"Yes."

"It would please me if you could stay longer. But you have your work to do, do you not?"

"I do."

"Tell me where you are going."

I took up a twig from the woodpile and scratched a rough map on the floor of the hut. She watched with interest as the map took form.

"Here is Macedonia," I said. "And here is Kavadar, and Skoplje, and Tetovo. And here"—a line to the south—"is the border between Greece and Yugoslavia. And the other parts of Yugoslavia—Croatia and Serbia and Bosnia-Hercegovina and Slovenia and Montenegro. You see, here is Belgrade, the capital."

"I see."

"And here to the east is Bulgaria, and above it Rumania. And west of Rumania is Hungary, and above it Czechoslovakia, and then Poland. You see?"

"Yes. You must go to Poland?"

"Farther than that. Here, above Poland and to the east, are three small countries. First Lithuania, then Latvia, then Estonia. They are all a part of Russia."

"So you go to Russia." She drew in her breath. "Is it not very dangerous to go to Russia?"

"They are a part of Russia in the same way that Macedonia is a part of Yugoslavia."

This she understood. "They too would fight for freedom," she said. "And you go to make a revolution there?"

"I hope not."

"Then, why else would you go there?"

"To get someone out of Latvia."

"It is difficult to leave Latvia?"

"It is nearly impossible."

"It will be dangerous?"

I told her that it would not be particularly dangerous. Evidently my voice lacked conviction, because she shot me a glance that told me she did not much believe me. But we dropped that subject and drank more of the fermented honey and talked of the struggles of Macedonia and the beauty of our son and the warmth of love.

After a while the boy woke up, crying lustily, and she fed him and put him back to sleep again. "Such a good boy," she said.

"He will need brothers and sisters."

"And we have worked to provide one for him."

"This is true," I said. "But can one be certain of the results?"

"I do not understand."

"When one wishes to grow a tree, one puts more than a single seed into the ground."

"We have planted two seeds already," she said, grinning.

"Would not a third seed make matters trebly sure?"

She purred. "You will be here several days. By the time you leave, I have a feeling that the ground will be overflowing with seeds."

"Would the ground object?"

"The ground shall have no objection."

"After all," I said, "one ought to leave as little as possible to chance."

"Especially when there is so much pleasure in the planting."

"This is true, too."

"I love you," she said.

And so we undressed a second time and moved again to her straw mattress and labored there most happily for the greater glories of Macedonia. Once more my marvelous son slept placidly through the joyous cries of love. And when it was over, I clung to her until she appeared to drift off to sleep. Then I drew away from her and covered her with blankets.

"I wish you could stay with me forever," she murmured.

"So do I."

"Why must you go to Latvia?"

"It's a long story," I said. And she stirred, as if prepared to ask for that long story, but instead she abruptly relaxed and this time she slept as peacefully as Todor.

I put my peasant clothing on once again and sat cross-legged in front of the fire, glancing now at my son and now at his mother, then turning my attention to the map I had drawn on the earthen floor. It would not do to leave the map there, I thought. Once I left Macedonia, it would be better if no one knew where I was going. I used another twig to obliterate the map, then pitched it into the fire and watched it burn.

*Why must you go to Latvia?*

A good question, a legitimate question. And my answer, while answering nothing, had surely been true enough.

It *was* a long story . . .

**18**

# 3

---------------------------------------------------------------

Karlis Mielovicius and I crouched in the shelter of a clump of scrub pine. Fifty-odd yards to our right a dozen riflemen crept resolutely forward. When they drew even with us, I extended one arm parallel to the ground. The men stopped in their tracks, then dropped to their knees and brought their rifles to bear upon the ramshackle wooden structure ahead of us. I held my arm out straight and counted to five, then dropped my arm abruptly.

A dozen rifles snapped in unison, peppering the clapboard building with a steady volley of shots. Karlis and I sprang into action. He yanked the pin from a grenade, counted as he ran, and hurled the grenade into the open doorway. I counted with him and ran at his side. Then, as the grenade sailed into the building, we both threw ourselves to the ground.

The explosion tore the little shed in half. The riflemen

were moving in now, firing as they ran, pouring bullets into the crippled shed. The gunfire dropped off as Karlis and I reached the doorway. I held up my arm again, and the rifle fire ceased entirely, and we went inside.

The shed was empty, of course. Had we been participating in an actual invasion of Latvia, the little building would have been strewn with the broken bodies of its defenders. But we were thousands of miles from Latvia. We were, to be precise, some five miles south and east of Delhi, in Delaware County, New York, where the Latvian Army-In-Exile was presently holding its annual fall encampment and field maneuvers.

"Mission accomplished," Karlis barked in Lettish. "Return to formation, double time."

The riflemen trotted back to their tents. Karlis broke out a pack of cigarettes and offered me one. I shook my head, and he lit one for himself. He smoked with the great gusto of a man who limits himself to three or four cigarettes a day and who consequently enjoys the hell out of the ones he smokes. He sucked great drags from the cigarette, inhaled deeply, held the smoke way down in his lungs, then expelled it all in a vast cloud.

"The men did well," he said.

"Very well."

"I was less pleased with the close-order drill, however. But our marksmanship is good, Evan, and our men work with enthusiasm. We may be pleased."

He was a huge, blond giant of a man, standing just over six and a half feet, weighing just over three hundred pounds. The U.S. Army might have had trouble finding a uniform to fit him. The Latvian Army-In-Exile had no such problem, as the dark green uniforms we all wore had to be individually tailored. Karlis's required rather more cloth than the rest, that's all.

Together we walked back to the tent we shared. It was the only tent in the entire encampment that had no beds in it. Since none of the army cots were long enough for him, Karlis preferred to take his king-size sleeping bag into the open and stretch out on the ground. I had no need for a bed, so on our first day in camp we'd had our double bunk carried away and moved in a pair of reasonably comfortable chairs. I sat in one, and Karlis sat in the other, and together we watched the sunset.

Karlis outranked me. He was a colonel in the Latvian Army-In-Exile, while I was a major. Our ranks may seem more impressive than they actually are. We have only officers in the army, no enlisted men. One aim of this form of organization is, admittedly, to provide our soldiers with the ego-gratification essential for an army in exile, but there is more to it than that. Our small group of men must be more than an effective fighting unit. Each of us will ultimately be called upon to command; when we invade Latvia, we will have to lead the workers and peasants and other patriots who flock to our standard. By providing every man with officer status, we will be better prepared to command our new recruits on the other side.

After all, there are only one hundred thirty-six of us, and we'll have our hands full.

Karlis stubbed out his cigarette on the sole of his boot, then automatically field-stripped the butt and scattered the shreds of tobacco to the wind. He balled the remaining bit of cigarette paper and flicked it away. Then he sat down again and sighed.

"Does something bother you, my friend?" I asked.

For a moment he seemed to hesitate. Then he said, "No, Evan. I am tired, that is all. Tomorrow we go home, and I will not be sorry to go."

We had been in camp for a full week. For seven days

21

we had spoken nothing but Lettish. For seven days we had arisen each morning at five and had put ourselves through a whole regimen of military activities, ranging from marching exercises to mock military operations, from classes and demonstrations in bomb-making and the use of various weapons to double-time marches with full field pack. We broke ranks each night for dinner, but the nights, while officially our own, were invariably given over to political discussions and songfests and folk dances. While an athlete like Karlis could stand up better than most under this sort of schedule, I could well appreciate that he would not be unhappy to return to Providence and the judo academy where he worked as an instructor.

A bugle blew, and we went to dinner. We ate well—the day's heavy exercise had provided almost everyone with a good appetite—and then we lingered over coffee until the women and girls of the Female Auxiliary made their appearance. It was the final night, and the program called for folk dancing around the bonfire and whatever additional delights might occur to various couples.

But Karlis had grown increasingly depressed. "I'm going to the tent," he announced.

"You won't stay for the dancing?"

"Not tonight."

"The girls are lovely," I said.

"I know. But it hurts my heart to see them. Lettish women are the most beautiful on earth, and the sight of them tears at my soul." His voice dropped to a conspiratorial level. "If you wish their company, I do not blame you in the least. But I have two bottles of French cognac in my knapsack. I have been saving them all week, and one of them is for you."

The girls *were* lovely, but many of them were wives and sweethearts, and there didn't look to be enough unattached

22

ones to go around. Besides, a week of hard work had taken its toll. Suddenly the thought of a good bottle of cognac held more appeal than the idea of dancing heroically around the campfire until one collapsed exhausted. I conveyed my feelings to Karlis, and together we headed back to our tent.

He found the two bottles, handed one to me, kept one for himself. We did not have glasses and made do without. We opened the bottles, offered the inevitable toasts in Lettish to the speedy liberation of Latvia from the yoke of Soviet domination and, that bit of formality safely out of the way, drank deeply from the bottles.

We put a good dent in both bottles before any real conversation got going. The moon was almost full, and we sat drinking in the moonlight and listening to the sounds of joy filtering through the night air from the campfire. Letts are good at having a good time, and the bunch around the campfire seemed to be doing just that. Letts are also accomplished at touching the very nadir of depression, and Karlis was drifting to that very point.

I have a touch of the chameleon about me. Had I stayed at the campfire, I would have joined in the fun. Now, in the moonlight with Karlis's cognac in me, I shared his mood. I became quite maudlin and ultimately I dragged out the charcoal sketch of my son Todor and showed it to Karlis.

"My son," I announced. "Is he not beautiful?"

"He is."

"And I have never seen him."

"How can this be?"

"He is in Macedonia," I said. "In Yugoslavia. And I have never returned since the night of his conception."

Karlis stared at me and at the picture, then at me again. And then, quite suddenly, he began to cry. He cried with his whole body, of which there was a great deal. His massive chest heaved with great sobs, and I remained respectfully

23

silent until he managed to regain control of himself.

And ultimately, his voice choked with emotion, he said, "Evan, you and I, we are more than fellow soldiers, we are more than comrades fighting together for a great cause. We are brothers."

"We are, Karlis."

"To have such a wonderful son and never to have seen him, that is a great tragedy."

"It is."

"I too have a tragedy in my life, Evan." He drank, and I drank. "It is this tragedy that keeps me from dancing with the lovely Lettish girls at the campfire. May I tell you of my tragedy?"

"Are we not brothers?"

"We are."

"Then, tell me."

He was silent for a moment or two. Then, his voice pitched low, he said, "Evan, I am in love."

Perhaps it was the cognac. Whatever the cause, I thought that those were the saddest and most poignant words I had ever heard. I began to weep, and now it was his turn to wait for me to get control of myself. After I had had another drink, he began to tell me about it.

"Her name is Sofija," he said softly. "And she is the world's most beautiful woman, Evan, with golden hair and the skin of a fresh peach and eyes as richly blue as the Baltic Sea. I met her at the Tokyo Olympics in nineteen sixty-four. You know that I represented the United States in the shot put."

"And placed second."

"Yes. I would have won but for that ox of a Georgian. Well, no matter. Sofija was there as a member of the Soviet Women's Gymnastic Troupe. No doubt you are aware that

24

the Baltic gymnasts are the finest in the world and that the Letts are superior to those in the other Baltic States."

I had not been aware of this.

"Sofija's team was victorious, of course. That such skill should be perverted to enhance the glory and prestige of the Soviet Union! Such grace, such liquid motion." He closed his eyes and sighed at the memory. "We met, Sofija and I. We met and we fell in love."

He stopped to light his fourth cigarette of the day. I had a feeling that this might be a night when he exceeded his tobacco ration. He smoked this cigarette all the way down, until he could not hold it without burning his fingers. Then he put it out and field-stripped it and then he had another long belt from the cognac bottle.

"You fell in love," I prompted.

"We fell in love. Sofija and I, we fell in love. Evan, my brother, it was not the sort of love to spend itself in a night or a week or a month. We truly loved each other. We wanted to have each other forever. We wanted to have children together, to grow old together, to become grandparents together, to remain together for all our lives." And his ears filled with his own words, and once again he began to weep.

"Did you ask her to defect?"

"Ask her? I begged her, I sank to my knees and pleaded with her. And it would have been so easy then, Evan. An easy ride to the American Embassy in Tokyo, a simple request for political asylum, and in no time at all the two of us would have been together in Providence. We would have been married, we would have had children, we would have grown old together, we would have had grandchildren together, we would have——"

"But she refused?"

"This," he said, "is the tragedy."

25

"Tell me."

"She *did* refuse at first. She is only a girl, Evan. She was twenty years old when we met. By the time of her birth Latvia had already been a part of the Soviet Union for three years, and the Russians were our allies in the struggle against German fascism. What did she know of a free and independent Latvia? She was raised in a little town some miles from Riga. She went to Russian schools and learned what Russian teachers taught her. She spoke Russian as well as she spoke Lettish, can you imagine? What could she understand of defecting? She wanted to be a patriot and did not understand what true Lett patriotism means. How could she comprehend the Soviet rape of the Baltic States? How could she know of this?

"So she refused. But love, Evan, love works powerfully upon Letts. When we fall in love, it is not a matter to be shrugged off. The games ended. We separated. I returned to the States, Sofija returned to Riga. And then, when it was too late, when it was no longer a simple matter of a taxi ride to the United States Embassy, then my Sofija attempted to defect. Her troupe was in Budapest for a gymnastic exhibition, and she tried to escape."

"In Budapest?"

He shrugged. "Of course it was absurd. She was captured immediately and returned to Russia. She was immediately expelled from the all-Soviet team to the team of the Latvian Soviet Socialist Republic, the L.S.S.R. Now, instead of touring the world, she plays matches with the teams of the other Soviet states. She does not leave Russia. She can never leave Russia. It is prohibited. She remains in Riga, and I remain in the States, and we go on loving each other and yet we can never be together." He took a long pull of cognac. "And that is my tragedy, Evan," he said. "That is my un-

26

happy little love story, that is my tragedy."

We drank, we cried, we drank, we sobbed, we drank. We discussed the utter impossibility of his situation, the unlikelihood of his ever finding another woman to replace Sofija, the slim chance that his love for her would ever fade away.

And at last he had an idea. "Evan, my brother," he said, "you are able to travel, are you not? You are skilled at that sort of thing?"

"How do you mean?"

"Oh, that you can slip in and out of this Iron Curtain. You have been to Macedonia, have you not?"

"To all of Yugoslavia," I said proudly. "And to Hungary and Czechoslovakia and Bulgaria. Never to Rumania or Albania or Poland. Or East Germany or Russia, of course."

"And never to Latvia?"

"No."

"But could you get to Latvia? They say that it is very difficult."

Blame it, if you will, on the cognac. For what I said was, "For the determined man, my brother Karlis, there is no such thing as a frontier. I have had some experience at this sort of thing. What, after all, is a border? An imaginary line that fools have drawn across the face of a map. A strand of barbed wire. A customs checkpoint. An experienced man, a capable man, can slip through any border like water through a sieve."

"Then, you could enter the Soviet Union."

"Of course."

"You could get into Latvia."

"I don't see why not."

He grew very excited. "You could take me with you," he said hurriedly. "You could show me the way, you could help me, and you could sneak me into Latvia and to Riga and reunite me with Sofija, and we would never have to be separated again."

"I . . . wait a minute."

He looked at me.

"You would return to Latvia?"

"I cannot live without Sofija, Evan. Better to live in slavery with Sofija than in Rhode Island without her."

"But your work with the Army——"

"I could be of even more assistance to the Army if I lived there. I could send bulletins back, I could do organizational work——"

"That's not what I meant, Karlis. Don't you understand? They know you there, they know of your work with the exile movement. You'd be arrested at once."

"I could disguise myself."

I looked at him dubiously.

"I could, Evan."

"As what? A tree? A mountain?"

"Evan, I cannot live without her!"

And then, because my cognac bottle was very nearly empty, and because what had been in the bottle was now in me, and because one's inability to sleep does not preclude the possibility that alcohol, in sufficient quantity, will addle the brain, I said something very stupid.

What I said was, "Karlis, you are like a brother to me. And Karlis, my brother, I can do much more for you than deliver you to slavery in Latvia. I can go to Latvia, Karlis, and I can find your Sofija and I can bring her back to you, and the two of you can then live in Providence for the rest of your lives, and you can get married, and you can have children together, and you can grow old together, and you can have grandchildren together, and——"

"You could do that, Evan?"

28

"I could."

"You could bring my Sofija to me?"

"I could. And I will."

If there is truth in wine, then there is also abject stupidity in brandy. From that point on, the night went as it had to go. Karlis assured me over and over again that I was the finest man on earth, a prince, a hero, a true and pure Lett. And eventually he got foggy enough to pass out, and I roused him just enough to lead him through the fields to his sleeping bag, where I helped him off with his uniform and tucked him off to sleep.

Then I walked around for a while in the cool air until something vaguely approaching sobriety returned. And at that point I realized just how absurd had been my promise to Karlis. I had never before attempted to get into Russia. I had never even contemplated the problem, nor had I considered the even greater problem of getting out once I had gotten in.

And now I had given my word that I would do just that. Not merely by myself, but that I would bring an unsuccessful defector out with me. This was so obviously impossible that it was really not worth thinking about.

Perhaps, I thought, the cognac would cancel out its own excesses. Perhaps when morning came, a weakened and hung-over Karlis Mielovicius would have blacked out the memory of the conversation and the ridiculous promise I had made him. Perhaps he would forget the whole thing.

He didn't.

We broke camp in the morning. I had a hangover, and Karlis had a hangover, and, as far as I could see, half the camp had a hangover. It seemed as though alcohol had flowed as freely at the folk dance as it had in our tent, although the mood there was jubilant, while ours had been maudlin.

But Karlis's words came through the hangover to me. "Evan, you will not forget what you said last night. You will go to Latvia, eh?"

I could have said no. The hell I could. I had built him up and I had to find the right way to let him down gently. This wasn't the time for it, or the place, or the mood.

"I'll do it," I said. "But it may take time——"

"I know, Evan."

"I'll have to do a great deal of planning. Some specific research. I'll have to get in touch with my Eastern European contacts."

"My love can wait, Evan."

I looked at that beaten blond giant and hated myself. By now, I thought, his girl was probably married to some petty commissar and enjoying the good life in revisionist Russia. Or, Lett that she was, she might still be torching for Karlis as he torched for her, consumed by this grand passion, with no hope of ever seeing him again.

I would stall him. What else could I do? I would stall him, and maybe someday he would forget about it. Or else, with time to let his hopes down slowly, he would simply realize that one could put little faith in the boasts and promises of a drunken Evan Tanner.

I went back to New York hating myself, and the hangover was only partially to blame.

# 4

-----------------------------------------------------------------

Back in New York, with my dark green Latvian uniform returned to storage for another year, and with the academic problems of a mixed bag of unscholarly scholars to occupy my time, Karlis and his love life assumed a bit less importance to me. I live in a four-and-a-half-room apartment on the fifth floor of an elevatorless old building on 107th Street a few doors west of Broadway. The four rooms are lined with floor-to-ceiling bookshelves (the half room is a kitchenette, and there's barely room to boil an egg in it), and the bookshelves are filled with books and pamphlets and magazines. There is a little-used bed in one room, and a dresser in another, and a desk in yet another, and there are chairs here and there.

I spend most of my time at the desk. My government pension barely covers the dues I pay to various organizations, let alone the cost of my magazine subscriptions, and

I make up the difference by writing theses and term papers for graduate and undergraduate students who are (a) too lazy or (b) too stupid or (c) both of the above. I generally have more work available than I care to handle; my rates are reasonable and my work is good, with a B-minus guaranteed. For several years I also took examinations for unprepared students, but I've dropped this recently. The challenge it once held has gone out of it, and only the tedium remains. A good doctoral thesis, on the other hand, takes quite a bit of meticulous research, all of which I hugely enjoy.

I had cleaned up a thesis on Lenin's views of the Paris Commune before heading upstate for the Latvian encampment and I took on two more assignments shortly after my return: a study of English class structure as represented in Jane Austen's novels and a shorter paper on the causes of the First Balkan War. These were easy topics for me, so much so that almost all of my footnotes were legitimate. I usually invent a large portion of them, but in this case it was hardly necessary. I wrote the papers and took my money.

And, in the course of all of this, I ate my usual five meals a day, sorted and read my mail, went to various meetings and lectures, listened to a set of Siamese language records—a difficult tongue, by the way, and a positively mind-freezing alphabet—and generally went about the business of life. Part of the business of life was the careful task of ignoring Karlis Mielovicius and his true love in Latvia.

This would have been easier if Karlis had not kept reminding me of my promise. He wasn't an absolute pest. On the contrary, he was so patient and understanding that I was soon consumed with guilt. But he filled my mailbox with little reminders—a picture of the girl, a letter he had received from someone who knew her, a variety of news clippings referring to Latvia, that sort of thing.

I suppose, with all of this gentle prodding, I would eventually have gone to Latvia anyway. It was senseless, certainly, but pure logic and reason make a bad foundation for a human life. One has to do idiot things from time to time, if only to assure oneself that one is a human being and not a robot.

So I probably would have gone anyway. But a couple of months after the encampment the Chief got in touch with me and ordered me to go to Colombia, and the next thing I knew I was on my way to Latvia.

I was heading home from an anarchist forum when the first contact was made. I left the subway at 103rd Street and walked north on Broadway, and at the corner of 106th a clean-cut young fellow tapped me on the shoulder.

"Excuse me," he said, "but I think you dropped this."

He handed me a crumpled piece of paper. "I don't think so," I said.

"I'm sure I saw you drop it," he said. "It might be important." And he pressed the piece of paper into my hand. Before I could say anything else he scurried off into the night.

I unfolded the scrap of paper. It was the wrapper from a piece of Juicy Fruit gum. I never chew gum and if I did I don't think I would chew anything called Juicy Fruit and if I did I'm sure I wouldn't save the wrappers. I dropped it in a litter basket and went home.

I didn't leave the apartment until noon the next day, at which time I decided that the restaurant down the block could outperform my own little kitchen. I left my building and walked to the corner of Broadway, and the clean-cut young fellow came up to me and tapped me on the shoulder.

"Excuse me," he said, "but I think you dropped this."

And handed me a crumpled piece of paper.

"It might be important," he said once again, a hint of

steel in his mellow voice. And off he went again. I went to the restaurant and ordered a plate of scrambled eggs and fried potatoes. I hadn't thrown away the scrap of paper this time. I felt it was definitely important. Either I was quietly losing my mind or someone was attempting to make contact with me, and the piece of paper seemed likely to hold a clue.

I uncrumpled it while I waited for them to scramble the eggs and fry the potatoes. It was a Juicy Fruit gum wrapper (the same one? a different one? who knows? and who cares?). This time I turned it over and found that someone had written something on the back.

Like this:

> *T:*
> *SP r-ints.*
> *Soonest.*

The scrambled eggs and fried potatoes came. I ate them. I drank several cups of coffee. I read the message over and over again. I would have to destroy it, I decided. It wouldn't do to leave it lying about where anyone could find it. Someone might glean information from it. Just because I couldn't get anything out of it didn't mean that some keen-eyed, quick-brained lad couldn't get a kernel of meaning out of it.

*Sprints.* No, correct that: *SP r-ints.*

Uh-huh.

The *T* seemed likely to mean Tanner. The *soonest* probably meant that I was supposed to do something right away. And the fundamental insanity of this particular method of delivering a message suggested the message's source. Only the undercover agencies of the United States Government operate habitually in this fashion.

Which meant that this gum wrapper was a message from the Chief. A certain amount of his cuteness is dictated by circumstances. Since I'm a subversive a couple thousand times over, my privacy is limited in certain ways. The FBI taps my phone and reads my mail before I do, and the CIA has bugged my apartment. Or perhaps it's the other way around. I'm not entirely sure which is which and I don't entirely care.

*SP r-ints?*

I tucked the gum wrapper into my shirt pocket and took it back to my apartment. I puzzled over it for a while, then hauled over the telephone and looked at the dial. Then I got it. *SP r-ints* was a telephone number. Just substitute the appropriate numbers for the last five letters and one came up with SPring 7-4687.

Which I did not dial just then, since either the CIA or the FBI was tapping my phone. Instead I left the building again and found a pay phone and invested a dime and dialed the number.

A girl said, "Good afternoon, Omicron Employment."

I said, "Tanner."

The girl said, "Room Two-one-oh-four, Hotel Crichton."

I said, "Soonest?"

The girl said, "At once."

I said, "How Mickey Mouse can you get?" but before saying that, I broke the connection.

And then I looked in the phone book and found out that the Hotel Crichton is on East 36th Street between Lexington and Third, and I took a cab to it and went all the way up to the twenty-first floor and found Room 2104 and knocked on the door and opened it when a voice suggested I do so and went inside.

And there he was.

•  •  •

He is a soft and rounded man with a bald head and fleshy hands and innocent blue eyes. He smiled me into a chair, filled a pair of water tumblers a third of the way with Scotch, gave one of them to me, and kept the other for himself. We drank.

"Ah, Tanner," he said. "You almost gave that lad a coronary when you threw away the gum wrapper last night. Put him a bit off stride."

"I guess I wasn't thinking."

"Figured out the phone number quickly enough, though. Sprints." He chuckled softly. "You would be surprised," he said, "just how many phone numbers can be converted into simple English words. A handy mnemonic device."

"Clever."

"Hmmm," he said.

I don't know his name. I think of him as the Chief because I've heard him called that, but I've never learned his name or his title or even the name of the agency he heads. Nor do I know how to get in touch with him should the occasion arise. I think he works out of Washington. I can't be sure. I know that one is never supposed to attempt to make contact with him. One waits for the mountain to come to Mohammed. Now and then the mountain rents a New York hotel room and sends a cryptic message.

"I have a piece of work for you, Tanner. Another touch of whiskey?"

"No, this is fine."

"Good, good. What do you know about Colombia?"

"The university?"

"No, no, the country. South America."

"Oh," I said. "Colombia."

"Mmmm." He got to his feet, walked over to the window, fiddled with the shade. I wondered whether he was merely playing with it or whether this action would set off an uprising in Indonesia. He stopped fooling with the shade and turned to face me. "Colombia. Know much about the place?"

"Yes."

"The political situation?"

"Yes."

"How about a specific organization—the Colombian Agrarian Revolutionary Movement?"

"I know the group."

"Thought you might." He smiled suddenly. "Just what I said to myself when this first blew our way. Said if there's a nut group somewhere, my boy Tanner knows about it. Knew right out of the box you'd be the perfect man for this job."

He thinks I work for him. He has ever right to think so. A while ago, shortly after the conception of my son Todor, I had a little trouble with the Central Intelligence Agency, and to save my neck I *invented* the Chief. I kept telling the CIA that I worked for another federal agency and couldn't tell them a thing about it. When the Chief appeared to rescue me, I was more surprised than the CIA was. I was also trapped by my own story. He thought I was one of his trusted agents, and maybe I am.

"The Colombian Agrarian Revolutionary Movement," he said. "Communist, wouldn't you say?"

"Not exactly."

"They're never *exactly* communist. Not until after they take power. Then the true colors show. We've been getting a great many rumbles out of Colombia. The news isn't good."

"Oh?"

"Looks as though the country's ripe for a revolution. The Colombian Agrarian Revolutionary Movement has been whipping up a lot of popular sentiment lately. From all

37

indications, they're planning a full-scale power play within the next two or three weeks. And that, Tanner, is where you come in."

I looked inquisitive.

"Your job," he said, "is to get inside this red group and stop it. Kill off the revolution. Nip it in the bud, squash it. We've got a friendly government in Colombia now——"

"A dictatorship."

"Well, that's a strong word, but let's just call it a friendly government. Colombia is an ally, and we'd like to preserve the status quo. That's policy, Tanner, and they make those decisions way upstairs." He chuckled again. "The CIA wanted this one, you know. The Agency likes this sort of job, but they haven't smelled so well in Latin America since the Bay of You-Know-Whats. And Edgar wanted this one, too. The Bureau swung a lot of weight in South America during War Number Two. But I knew you'd be the right man. A nice neat inside job, that's the way to kill the weed before it blooms." Another inane chuckle. "I'll never forget what you did in Macedonia. If you're as good at stopping revolutions as you are at starting them, this should be a cinch for you."

I finished my drink. He had a job for me, did he? A job that would be just right for me, was it?

I wouldn't touch it with a rake.

Because it just so happens that I am a member of the Colombian Agrarian Revolutionary Movement. I've supported CARM for several years and I've been able to donate some fairly substantial sums to them toward their end of overthrowing the Colombian Government. My contributions have been mostly financial, as there's very little CARM activity in the New York area. It is an activist movement, a rebel band that roams the Colombian hills, adding new recruits and gathering its strength for the uprising.

Communist? I knew CARM well and long, and I couldn't call them that. They are left-wing socialists, but their program is based in Colombia, not in Moscow or Peking or even Havana.

The news that a CARM revolution was imminent was welcome news indeed. The thought that I might be ordered to sabotage this revolution was terrifying. I would not do it. I would not dream of doing it. If I went to Colombia, it would be to *aid* the revolution, not to destroy it.

"I'm sorry," I said. "I can't go."

"What's that?"

"I can't go to Colombia. I can't accept the assignment."

"But that's ridiculous, Tanner. Why not?"

I killed time with a sip of Scotch. I finished the drink and while he poured more whiskey into my glass and his I shuffled through my brain looking for a convenient lie. I thought of those star-crossed lovers, Karlis and Sofija, and I stopped shuffling. If I had to do something ludicrous, I might as well do it in a good cause. If I had to go traipsing around the world, I might better traipse to Latvia than to Colombia.

I said, "There's another trip I have to take."

"Where to?"

"Eastern Europe."

"Be more specific."

"The Baltic States."

"Which one?"

"Does it matter?"

He stared intently at me. I was playing a dangerous game, but I had a hunch I might get away with it. From what I knew about his agency (*our* agency?), one had a considerable amount of leeway. His men did not make written reports or follow instructions. They were given a job to do, they made their own plans and established their own contacts, and they went in and did it and came back and announced that it was done. Or they didn't come back, and the Chief drank a toast to their memory.

"The Baltic States," he said.

"Yes."

"An important mission?"

"Not government business, really. A favor for a friend."

"Oh, come now, Tanner!"

I shrugged.

"I'm afraid I know you too well for that, Tanner. You wouldn't miss a chance at the Colombian job unless it were something very big indeed. There's a missile center outside of Tallinn. Is that part of it?"

"I'd rather not say anything in advance."

"Mmmm. Something bigger than Colombia. You won't tell me what it is?"

"Let me just say that it's an errand for a friend."

He chuckled again, and I knew everything was going to be all right for the time being. "You and Dallmann," he said. "You work best when you make your own plays. One of the best things Dallmann ever did was recruit you." Dallmann, who was dead, could be counted on not to set the record straight. "Well, I'm sorry I can't use you in Colombia. We don't have anyone else handy who could turn the trick. I'll have to hand it back to the Agency. Who knows? They might even do something right for a change."

On the way home I stopped at the Western Union office. I wired a friend in Bogota. I sent the message in Spanish, but in English it would work out to something like this: BEST OF LUCK IN COMING VENTURE. UNDERSTAND BOY SCOUTS ARE COMING. TAKE CARE.

That night I took a train to Providence.

Karlis gave me her picture and her address and his blessing. He wanted desperately to come along, and it was not

40

easy to talk him out of it. I kept reminding him that the Russians would know of his high position with the Latvian Army-In-Exile and that his presence in the country would endanger not only himself but me and Sofija in the bargain. He was disappointed, but he could appreciate the truth of that.

"The entry and escape will be difficult," I told him. They would be impossible, I thought. "And I must travel as light as possible. One man, alone, might be able to get in. One man and one woman might be able to get out. But I won't even take a suitcase, just a few things in a leather portfolio. I want to travel light."

I didn't want to travel at all. But I went home again and packed some things in my slim satchel and I studied maps of Europe and I thought of flying straight to Helsinki. Finland is just across the Baltic from Estonia, and that would be the simplest way of entering the region.

Then I remembered my son Todor. And for the first time the trip's *être* had a *raison*. I couldn't expect to rescue Sofija because that was plainly impossible. I could not honestly expect to get into Latvia at all. But I could damn well get into Yugoslavia and I could find Annalya and I could see my son.

The next morning, bright and early, I caught a TWA jet to Athens.

# 5

----------------------------------------------------------------

For three days and three nights I lived the good life in Macedonia. I gathered wood for the fire. I played with Todor and sported with Annalya. I cut myself a hardwood walking stick and took long treks over the rugged hillside. I breathed air a thousand times fresher than the black murk that hangs over New York. I drank pure spring water and fresh goat's milk. I ate thick black bean soup and roasted lamb. I entertained fleeting thoughts of the ease with which I might go native, raising a thick and drooping Macedonian moustache, tending a brace of goats, and remaining forever with my ready-made family. In the cool, clean air of Macedonia, Riga and Manhattan seemed equally remote, equally nonessential to my personal happiness.

But one sun-brightened morning it was time. I looked at Annalya, and she looked at me, and her eyes clouded. She said, "Today?"

"Yes."

"You must go, then? It is time?"

"It is time, little dove."

"I am a Macedonian woman," she said, "and will not weep."

There was nothing to pack. I tucked my slim satchel between two of my sweaters. I picked up my walking stick. Annalya came to me, and we kissed and held each other. Todor, alone upon his mattress, was but a young Macedonian; he cried, and Annalya picked him up and brought him to me. I held him up in the air and grinned at him, and he stopped crying.

"He is a good boy," I said. "I am proud of him."

"He brings me joy."

"I am grateful for the picture of him. If, from time to time, you could have other pictures drawn and sent to me——"

"It shall be done."

When I reached the door she said, "You will return, Evan?"

"Yes. Someday."

"Perhaps Todor shall have many brothers."

I turned to her, and saw the radiance of her eyes and the set of her jaw and the great strength and beauty of her. And Latvia, after all, was miles and miles away over cold and distant lands. So I reentered the hut and closed the door, and we put Todor to sleep on his own little straw mattress, and it was another warm, sweet hour before I got out of there.

The map I had drawn on the floor of the hut remained brightly outlined in my mind. While I worked my way north through Yugoslavia I spent my time planning the route I would have to take. There was a simple way to do it, one

**44**

that would involve crossing only two borders. I could cross from Yugoslavia to Rumania and from Rumania to the Soviet Union and then, once inside Russia, I could make my way north to Latvia. That cut down on the border hopping, but it also meant I would have to travel a great distance within the confines of the Soviet Union.

I was not especially anxious to do this. From what I understood, internal security within Russia is honed to a keener edge than in the Eastern European satellite nations. Even the police in countries like Hungary and Poland will occasionally overlook subversive activity on the grounds that it is not so much anti-Hungarian or anti-Polish as it is anti-Russian. The Russian authorities, on the other hand, cannot gift themselves with this convenient excuse, and a conspirator's lot is proportionately more difficult there.

That was only part of it. The political crazy quilt of Eastern Europe was dotted with friends and comrades of mine, political oases in a desert of officialdom. And, while I had a smattering of such friends in Russia itself, notably my Armenian Nationalist friends in the south and a handful of Ukrainians and White Russians, they were scattered far and wide and came under rather close government scrutiny.

A final factor: I had never been to Russia. The new and unknown carries its own special terrors.

I planned my route. North through Yugoslavia to Belgrade, the capital. On into Hungary, bypassing Budapest to the east. Cutting across Czechoslovakia at the extreme eastern corner of Slovakia, and on into Poland with a stopover at either Krakow or Lublin. Then due north through Poland to Lithuania, and onward from Lithuania to Latvia, and then—

Then home again, home again, jiggety-jig.

Of course I would have to find a simpler and more direct route home. If I actually did manage to get into Latvia, I could go home via Finland. If I found it too hazardous to cross into Russia—and this certainly seemed likely—I could choose between crossing the sea from Poland to Finland or Sweden or working my way westward through Germany and France. Any of these possible courses would take a good long time, and time was one thing I had in abundance. If nothing else, I had to stay out of the States long enough for the CARM revolution to take place. It would probably fail—the vast majority of revolutions do—but if it failed, at least it would do so without my having contributed to its defeat.

Meanwhile I was in Yugoslavia, a political absurdity, the last stronghold of prewar Balkan nationalism, an ill-sorted lot of Serbs and Croats and Slovenes and Bosnians and Montenegrins and Macedonians, of Stalinists and revisionists and anarchists and monarchists and social democrats and assorted unclassifiable madmen, all nestled among jagged mountains and pea-green valleys and winding blue rivers.

I love Yugoslavia.

Once I had reached Belgrade, it was no particular problem to find Janos Papilov's house. I had been there before on a trip that had led south through Yugoslavia, and his house was still the same, dark and unimposing on the outside, immaculate and tastefully furnished within. Janos himself met me at the door with a smile and a firm handshake. No rough embraces; Janos, Professor of Indo-European Languages at the University of Belgrade, is a man of infinite culture and sophistication. He led me to the dining room, where his wife and father-in-law were seated. There was a place already set for me.

"You see," he said, "I knew that you were coming, my friend." He smiled at my surprise. "In my country," he said, "news travels even faster than an American *agent provocateur*. But be seated, Evan. There will be the whole night for conversation. May I strongly recommend the wine? It is Slovenian, the sort of dry white wine they do rather well there. You might almost mistake it for a Moselle."

We gossiped pleasantly during dinner. A fairly important officer of the New York chapter of the Serbian Brotherhood had been involved in an amusing scandal with another brother's wife, and Janos was hungry for details. Some of the details, and some of his comments upon them, were not entirely suited for the ears of Mrs. Papilov or her father, so our conversation was not conducted exclusively in Serbo-Croat. Janos' wife spoke French and Russian and a little English. But Janos himself spoke all of the major European languages and a few others as well, and the conversation bounced from one tongue to another, from Rumanian to Hungarian to Greek, as we elaborated upon the strange bedfellows that politics makes.

After dinner Janos led me to his study. He was a long, lean man, with sparse gray hair and thick wire-rimmed spectacles. He sat at his desk, and I sat in a comfortable leather chair, and for a few moments we chatted idly of political friends. Then the conversation ran out of momentum, and he sat back in his desk chair and regarded me thoughtfully.

"It is providential that you have come at this time," he said finally.

"Why?"

"Because there is something you must read. Something you will find quite fascinating."

"A book?"

"A manuscript for a book."

"Yours?"

"No." He smiled briefly. "I have a book coming out soon

on the dialects of the Ukraine, but I would not press such a weighty tone upon you."

"I'd be most interested——"

"You are kind to say so, and rest assured that I will send you a copy upon publication. But the manuscript I have for you is most important, believe me. Are you too tired to read it now?"

"Not at all."

He opened the desk's center drawer and drew out a large manila envelope. From the envelope he brought forth a sheaf of typescript. "The text is in Serbo-Croat," he said. "But if you read as fluently as you speak, that should present no problem."

"I read Serbo-Croat."

"Then you'll finish this in an hour or so if you're a fast reader. Don't read for detail. Merely read carefully enough to form an opinion of the merit of the work."

I took the manuscript from him. There was no title page. I asked the author's name.

"I will tell you when you finish."

"And the title?"

"The work is yet untitled. Perhaps you will be more comfortable at my desk. Please sit here, I'll leave you alone while you read. And would you care for a cup of coffee?"

"Fine."

I sat down expecting the usual sort of Serb propaganda, perhaps a bit better than the general run if Janos was so impressed. But within the first few pages I saw that the book was a far cry from the normal class of partisan literature. It was, in fact, an astonishing document. With an impartial viewpoint almost without precedent in Balkan political literature, the author made a rational yet impassioned plea for the dissolution of the state of Yugoslavia and the establishment of wholly independent republics of Croatia,

Slovenia, Serbia, Macedonia, and Montenegro.

It could have been mere polemic, but the man who wrote it had avoided this pitfall. Every charge leveled at the People's Republic of Yugoslavia was carefully thought out and as carefully documented. Every argument for the Yugoslav federation was meticulously examined and meticulously demolished. The successes of Tito's revisionist policies paled to the point of insignificance under the weight of the author's charges.

And all of this was done, not from the point of view of a diehard Croat or Serb or Slovene, but with genuine scholarly detachment.

I found Janos working chess puzzles in the living room. "The book is a masterpiece," I told him.

"I thought you would be impressed. You feel it deserves publication?"

"Of course."

"But," he said, "I find it unlikely that it would be published in Yugoslavia. If Djilas can earn imprisonment for his writings——"

"This author would hang."

"Precisely."

"The book could be published in America."

"Ah. And then what would happen to its author?"

"The book could be published anonymously. Or under some convenient pen name."

"Perhaps. But I have a feeling that this author's name might carry weight."

"Who is he?"

"You approve wholeheartedly of the book? Of its style? Of its message?"

"Yes. Without reservation."

"You would even, perhaps, be willing to translate it into English?"

**49**

"I would be honored."

"Ah. The author, as it happens, is a gentleman by the name of Milan Butec."

"You don't mean——"

"Deputy Minister of Internal Affairs of the People's Republic of Yugoslavia. Precisely. A resistance leader during the war. An important organizer of Tito's government after the war. A respected man, a leader, a scholar, a thinker—"

"The book must be published," I said. "And of course you are right, it ought to be issued under Butec's name. Someone must find a way to get the man out of Yugoslavia to safety in the West. This is imperative."

"I agree."

"And if this is done, I would be honored to translate the work."

Janos Papilov sighed. "You will do more than that, Evan," he said. "Do you not recall that I said your visit was providentially timed? Early today I received word that you were en route to Belgrade. Perhaps it was presumptuous of me, but I took it for granted that you would visit me upon your arrival. And so I immediately got word to Mr. Butec, whose manuscript has been in that drawer of my desk for over a month. He came to my house this afternoon; he has been waiting in an upstairs room since your arrival."

"May I meet him?"

Another sigh. "You may do much more than meet him, Evan. It will be your task to take Mr. Butec and his most valuable manuscript to America."

For a few moments I said nothing. Extreme shock often has that effect upon me. Then I said, "Janos, you honor me. But what you ask is impossible. I'm not on my way home now. I have to go north, I have to travel through

Hungary and Czechoslovakia and Poland——"

"Mr. Butec will travel with you."

"Janos, I have to enter Russia!"

"That is very dangerous. But it would be still more dangerous for Mr. Butec to remain in this country. He has been cautious not to make his view publicly known. He has been most discreet. Still, word of his writings has somehow leaked to the government. Three days ago he was placed under unofficial house arrest. This afternoon he left his house by climbing down the drainpipe and running through backyards like a petty burglar. He must leave Yugoslavia at once."

"Then let him leave by himself. Or let someone else take him."

"It is impossible, Evan."

"But——"

"Milan Butec has no experience in these matters. He could not go alone. Nor is there anyone whom we trust, anyone with the ability to escort Mr. Butec. But you, Evan, you slip in and out of countries with ease. Are you permitted in Yugoslavia? You are not. Yet how often have you come in and out of this country illegally?"

"But I travel light," I protested. "I didn't even bring a suitcase this time, just a flat portfolio that I can slip inside my jacket. I'd be hampered if I had to take the manuscript with me, let alone its author. And I'm not going west, Janos. I'm going north and east."

"They will not expect that," he said, undaunted.

"Of course they won't. They'll expect him to do the sensible thing and sneak out through Austria or Greece."

"Exactly. And those are the frontiers they will guard, while you——"

"I can't do it, Janos."

"You must. Would you want this book suppressed? Would you want the author hanged?"

"Janos . . ."

We went around and around, Janos and I. I thought of countless alternatives and he explained at length why each one was unthinkable, why no one else could possibly take Butec to freedom, why Butec could not possibly go himself. We went around and around, and so did my head. The whole mission to rescue Sofija for Karlis had been impossible to begin with, but if I traveled light, I had the chance, say, of a snowball in hell. With Butec and his book in tow, even that much chance was denied me. He would be wanting to sleep all the time. He wouldn't know the languages. He would get in the way, he would do something wrong.

Damn . . .

"You will come with me, Evan," Janos said at last. "We will meet Mr. Butec."

"Janos——"

"Come!"

Mr. Butec, Mr. Milan Butec, Deputy Minister of Internal Affairs for the People's Republic of Yugoslavia, was a short and stout man with a neatly trimmed goatee, huge bushy eyebrows, and a hairless head. My heart sank when I saw him; he would be about as inconspicuous as a Negro in the D.A.R.

"This is Evan Michael Tanner," Janos said. "This is the young man, Milan, who has agreed to lead you to freedom and to give the world the gift of your most precious book."

This was a lie; I had agreed to nothing. But Butec—and what a fine book he had written, what a masterful book—scurried over to pump my hand. He tried to express his gratitude in English. His accent was thicker than Macedonian bean soup.

"It will be difficult," I heard myself say.

"I am prepared for difficulty."

52

"And dangerous."

"I am prepared for dangerous."

Prepared for dangerous? I swung us back to Serbo-Croat. "And you would have to disguise yourself, Mr. Butec." I studied him, trying to think of a way to make him look a little less obviously himself. "A wig of some sort, I should think. And you would have to shave your beard. Perhaps the eyebrows as well, and then we would paint in less obtrusive eyebrows."

"This shall be done as you say."

He stroked his beard as he said this, and I knew he was vain about it. I only wished he was vain enough to offer an objection and leave me with a way out, but evidently his vanity placed second to his desire to see the last of Yugoslavia.

I said, with the heavy heart of one who goes on playing even after he knows he has lost, "It will be a hard trip, Mr. Butec. We will have to be on the move constantly. There won't be much time for sleep and——"

Butec managed a smile. "Do not worry," he said. And, drawing himself up to what there was of his full height: "Put your mind at ease in that department, Mr. Tanner. I can put up with such hardship. I have trained myself to make do with almost no sleep at all."

Well, I thought, that was a help.

"There are times," he added, "when I get by with as little as six hours sleep a night."

"That's marvelous," I said.

# 6

-------------------------------------------------------------

When Milan Butec emerged from the lavatory, a straight
razor clasped defensively in one hand and a valiant smile
on his round white face, he had been all too literally shorn
of the last vestiges of human dignity. The bald head gleamed
as before, but now the beard was gone as well, revealing
a weak chin. The missing eyebrows gave the whole head
the uncanny appearance of a round ball of soft white cheese,
indented here and there for eyes and a mouth, protruding a
bit for a nose, but otherwise scarcely identifiable as a human
head at all. The poor man evidently had a mad passion for
escape; only that or abject masochism would permit a man
to make such a profound mess of himself.

"I am not looking myself," he said.

Janos maintained a tactful silence. His wife said something about coffee and retreated to the kitchen. Milan Butec
and I regarded each other thoughtfully. With some sort of

wig, I thought, and with rudimentary eyebrows drawn in to interrupt some of the awesome expanse of white skin, he would still look rather absurd. But he would look not at all like Milan Butec.

"We will need a wig," I told Janos.

"This can be arranged. Black, do you think?"

"Perhaps a dark brown."

"I shall see to it. What else?"

"An eyebrow pencil. If there's nothing of the sort available, perhaps some charcoal or a burnt match——"

"Cosmetics are a petit bourgeois artifice not in keeping with the goals and ideals of a socialist nation," Janos said solemnly. "My wife has several eyebrow pencils. You will want to take one with you, of course. It shall be provided."

"And peasant clothing, something along the lines of what I am wearing. Milan Butec is an intellectual and a political leader. Dressed as a peasant, he will be less apt to be recognized."

Janos assured me that appropriate garments of the correct size could be readily obtained. He could also furnish auto transportation to within a few miles of the frontier. From that point on, he said, we would be on our own.

We went to the kitchen and sat over cups of thick black coffee. Mme. Papilov excused herself once, returned with an eyebrow pencil, excused herself a second time and went away. Janos left us with the explanation that he would get hold of a wig and arrange for transportation immediately after breakfast the next morning. I poured fresh coffee for Butec and myself and fortified both cups with a tot of brandy.

"I know I am trouble for you," he said. "I regret."

"It is no trouble."

"You are kind." He stroked the air an inch from his chin, caressing where a beard had been for thirty years or so, then caught himself and stared at his hand. "Habits," he said.

56

"Men are so much the creatures of habit."

"Yes."

"I have spent over twenty years as a scholar, a bureaucrat, a political minister. But before this, you know, I was with the Partisans. I was a resistance leader in the war against fascism. I gave orders, and men followed my command."

"It was a heroic fight, and——"

"Please. My point is not to win applause for my actions of years past. It is simply that you should know that I appreciate the nature of command, of one man leading and another man taking orders. In this little expedition of ours you are clearly in command. You are the expert. I am the novice. Whatever orders you give, I am prepared to follow." He paused, looked down at himself, and patted his plump stomach and short legs. "You, on the other hand, must appreciate that to order me to swim the English Channel or scamper across the Sahara Desert would be a difficult order for me to execute."

He said all of this quite straight-faced, then let his face relax into the first smile he had shown me.

"We may cross the Baltic Sea," I said. "But not under our own power."

I filled my own coffee cup again. He covered his own with his hand, explaining that he wanted to be able to get to sleep. "One final point," he said. "You are of course familiar with the old medical problem, whether the doctor shall save the life of the mother or the child when only one can be preserved. Some say that the younger generation should be shown preferential treatment. Others argue that a mother can have more children, while a child would have difficulty gaining a second mother. But in my case it is important that you realize the proper order of things. You understand the parallel, of course?"

"Your manuscript."

"Yes. The book is my child. My only child. Your first duty is to that child, Mr. Tanner. The child must reach the West. If you can save the mother as well"—a quick flash of smile—"so much the better, and my eternal gratitude. But if one must be sacrificed, let it be me. I would rather live in my writing than in my flesh. Words endure longer."

He rinsed out his cup at the sink, then headed for his bedroom, determined to prove that he could exist on a scant six hours of sleep. I put my own cup aside and had a short glass of brandy. He would, I knew, be at least as much of a burden as he thought he would be and probably a great deal more. But he was a man of valor and vision and a man who could hold on to a hard core of dignity no matter how undignified his appearance. Slipping him across one border after another seemed frankly impossible but not too much more so than the comparably herculean task of smuggling the comely Sofija from Riga, Latvia, to Providence, Rhode Island.

Janos came back with a bundle of peasant clothing that looked like simple peasant clothing, and a dark brown wig that looked exactly like a wig. I took these things and Butec's manuscript and the rest of the jug of brandy to my room and I sat around reading and drinking and planning while the rest of the household squandered six hours in sleep.

The manuscript, Milan Butec's only child, ran to nearly 300 pages of typescript. The first order of business was to affix it to my person in such a way that I would have nothing to carry—and, consequently, nothing to lose or misplace. I cut up some oilcloth that had previously lined the bureau drawers in my room and I divided the manuscript into four sections and sewed each batch of script into a double wrapping of oilcloth. While I didn't expect to swim either the

English Channel or the Baltic Sea, it seemed wise to protect the script from water damage.

I found a roll of heavy adhesive tape in the bathroom cabinet. In my own room I stripped to the skin and used the tape to attach the four packets to my body. I taped one around each thigh, one to my back and one to my chest. I dressed again, and there were no discernible bulges where I had taped the packets. I crinkled a bit when I moved around, but one gets accustomed to that sort of thing.

In a more orderly world, of course, the entire book would have been handily transcribed unto a single spool of microfilm, which I could have swallowed in Belgrade and defecated in New York. Such a triumph of technology would have saved me the necessity of strapping oilcloth packets all over my person and would have been perfectly safe from anything but a sudden attack of rampant colitis. No doubt the professional secret agents arrange things in such a way, and the pudgy man from Washington may have expected as much from me. But I do not have microphones in my shoes or cameras in my tie clasp or innocent-looking fountain pens that dispense deadly gases in lieu of ink. One must make do with the materials at hand.

I tucked the charcoal sketch of Todor into a pocket. It was the only item in my leather satchel with which I was not perfectly ready to part company. I committed Sofija's address to memory and studied her photograph until I felt qualified to pick her out of a rather small crowd. I incinerated the photo and the address in an ashtray, added the few books I'd brought along to Janos Papilov's bookshelves, and left the slim leather satchel on the bed. I made the brandy last, and by the time it was gone, the rest of the house was awake, and it was time for breakfast.

Milan Butec came fully awake about the same time he finished his third cup of breakfast coffee. He had dressed himself in the peasant clothing Janos had provided, and it fit him surprisingly well. Janos' wife drew in an acceptable pair of eyebrows, and I observed the process with interest; it was a task I would have to perform every time Butec washed his face. The eyebrows made an immediate difference, transforming him at once from Martian to human.

The wig helped too, but there was no getting away from the fact that it looked very much like a wig. Janos had not been able to get hold of any spirit gum, so we had to make hinges of adhesive tape and use them to affix the wig to Butec's scalp.

Butec looked at the result in the mirror and paled at what he saw.

"In the West," I said, "you will be able to grow the beard again."

"Of course."

"And dispense with the wig and let your eyebrows grow in naturally."

"Of course. But in the meantime the less often I have to look at a mirror . . ."

Janos revealed an unexpected talent for barbering, using a pair of paper shears to give the wig a quick trim that made it conform somewhat better to the shape of Butec's head. It still looked like a wig to me, but at least it looked like a well-chosen wig. With a cap covering most of it, the effect was greatly improved. Now, at least, he looked like a peasant.

But he didn't walk like one and he didn't talk like one, and all of this took coaching. The three of us worked out a blitz course in Instant Rustic Clod, with me as the teacher, Butec as the earnest pupil, and Janos as the critical observer. He had to exchange his military bearing and crisp stride and erect stance for the slouching, rolling gait of the peasant who knows how to cover many miles in a day. He had to train himself to mutter and mumble with the air of one who has learned throughout his life that no one is very interested in anything he might have to say.

It was no simple role for him to pick up in so short a time. I thought of that English king—one of the Henrys, I think the Second—who was supposed to have donned rustic garb and passed incognito among his subjects from time to time. I doubt that he really fooled many of them. But Butec, though hardly a natural actor, had the sort of practical mind that enabled him to know what he could manage and what was beyond his grasp. He would talk as little as possible, he assured me, and he would use the simplest possible words, and he would do his best to be a man whom no one would favor with a second glance.

By the time a wheezing, belching automobile came around to carry us to the border, he was ready.

The border between Yugoslavia and Hungary is an easy one. Whenever there is an extensive land frontier separating two countries, it is virtually impossible to patrol the border effectively. When a river forms the boundary, one may establish customs stations at the bridges. But Yugoslavia and Hungary have a long common border, and except for the central stretch where the Drava River divides the two countries, the border is not a geographical entity at all but merely a line on a map. The few roads that cross from one country to the other have customs posts. Between the roads there is nothing more imposing than a pair of wire fences thirty yards apart.

Our driver took us in nervous silence to within a dozen miles of the border, dropping us on the road that led from Velika Kikinda to the Hungarian town of Szeged. We walked northwest along the little-used road, and Butec showed that he had learned his lessons rather well. His legs relaxed into the easy gait of the Yugoslav peasant, and his eyes watched the ground ahead of him.

A few miles from the border we abandoned the road and cut east through a vineyard. Mme. Papilov had given us each a paper sack containing rolls and cheese and sausages, and I had tucked a flask of brandy into a hip pocket. We walked out of sight of the road and squatted among the grapevines to eat lunch. The grapes were not entirely ripe, but their tart taste was not unpleasant. We incorporated a few handfuls of them in our lunch.

When the food was gone, we nipped at the brandy and sat enjoying the feel of the hot noonday sun on our hands and faces. Butec the peasant looked years younger than Butec the politician. He sighed, smothered a belch, yawned, then stretched out flat on his back with his hands beneath his head. I thought for a bad moment that he was ready for another six hours of sleep. Then he began to talk.

"This is good for me," he said. "This fresh air, this good, plain food, this exercise. Is it not a beautiful day?"

"It is."

"And beautiful countryside?"

"Yes."

"The countryside where I was born is still more beautiful. You have been to Tzerna Gora?"

Tzerna Gora is Serbo-Croat for Montenegro. I told him that I had passed through the province several times.

"Do you know, perhaps, a town called Savnik?"

"I know of it, but I have never been there."

"I was born in Savnik. Not in Savnik itself but in a cottage a few miles from Savnik. So one might say that I am a human being, or a European, or a Yugoslav, or a Montenegrin, or simply a man of Savnik. Every man has many such identities, depending upon the breadth of one's view."

I said nothing.

"Do you believe, Mr. Tanner, that Montenegro ought to be free and independent?"

"Yes."

"Why?"

"For many of the reasons advanced in your book."

"And for others?"

"Perhaps." I prefer not to go into detail regarding my political beliefs. Too many persons would see my loyalties as being at odds each with the other. While I myself do not find this inconsistency bothersome, explanations tend to be tedious.

"You enjoyed my book, Mr. Tanner?"

"Very much."

"And approved of its contents?"

"So much so that I would be honored to translate it."

"It is you who would honor me. But, Mr. Tanner, did it occur to you to wonder why I wrote this book?"

"Out of conviction, I would guess. And to further the cause of separate republics in place of the Yugoslav Federation and——"

He interrupted me with a shake of his head. "Greater reasons than those, Mr. Tanner," he said. "And lesser ones also. But the most important reason of all, I would say, is that I do not care for war. I have been in war. I have killed men, I have seen men die around me. I do not care for war at all."

He took a small sip of brandy. "But war has always been with us, and I would suspect it will always continue to be. I know what war has been in the past. I have studied history all my life, Mr. Tanner, and I know the growing patterns of war, with ever larger countries pitting ever larger armies against one another. You know the poem 'Dover Beach'? An English poet, Matthew Arnold. I recall one line. 'Where ignorant armies clash by night.' All armies are ignorant,

Mr. Tanner, and all warfare takes place in the night of the soul.

"Now we have a world of huge countries, do we not? China, Russia, the United States, the Common Market of Western Europe, the Socialist nations of Eastern Europe. Large nations and combinations of nations. Years ago when two small countries fought a war, a man of peace could go fifty miles away and be in another country entirely and then he would not have to concern himself over the war. Little countries fought little wars, and little armies fought little battles, and the world went on. But imagine a war today between America and Russia, or America and China, or Russia and China. Where would a man go? Where would a man hide? And what would become of the world?"

I plucked a handful of grapes and munched them thoughtfully. It was time to move on, time to head for the border. But he was speaking well, and I wanted to hear him out without spoiling the mood.

"It is easy to imagine Yugoslavia divided into five or six republics. But now imagine China divided into two dozen provinces, and imagine your own country separated into fifty independent states, and the Soviet Union carved up in similar fashion. Then there could be no large wars, Mr. Tanner. Then there could be no men in positions of great power, and when a man of peace saw a war coming, he could move from one village to another and be untouched by the little war." He sighed heavily, then sat up. "So this is why I wrote my book, you see. Not because I expect the Yugoslav Federation to dissolve itself, but because I am an old man tired of war who is, when all is said and done, a native of Savnik who would like to die decently in Savnik, away from the cares of the world."

Milan Butec got to his feet. "But that is far too philosophical a speech for a sturdy Slavic peasant, is it not? And it is time that I returned to the role of the peasant. Let us go."

And we walked, he and I, like happy peasants, through the rows of grapevines toward the Hungarian border.

# 7

--------------------------------------------------------------

The fence on the Yugoslav side of the border stood eight feet tall, the bottom seven feet composed of dense steel mesh, the top foot a menacing weave of barbed wire. Some thirty yards beyond this fence was its Hungarian counterpart, perhaps a foot or so taller. Between them was a gravel-laden stretch of no-man's-land marked by the tire tracks of patrolling sentries. The fence was not electrified, which was about all that could be said in its favor. The mesh afforded little in the way of a toehold, and as far as I could see in either direction, there were no trees anywhere near the fence. The great expanse of vineyard offered nothing upon which to stand in order to scale the fence.

"You have a plan, Evan?"

We had progressed to first names. We had made inestimable progress generally, until this damned fence had come along. No, I told him, I did not have a plan.

"Could we cut our way through the mesh?"

"I don't have a wire-cutter with me. Besides, it would take hours. I could boost you over, Milan."

"But how would you get over?"

I didn't answer him. I thought about cutting back to the road and trying to bluff our way through the border station. I might have tried it alone, but I didn't dare with Butec along for company. The stakes were too high, and he was too new at the game.

"A ladder," I said. "Stakes."

"Pardon?"

"These vines are staked, aren't they? Let's see what the stakes look like." I went to one of the grapevines, tugged it loose from its supporting stake, then yanked the stake free of the soil. It was about four feet long, two inches wide, and an inch thick. I carried it over to the fence and wedged it into the mesh. Angled slightly, it went in rather nicely.

"We'll need a dozen of these," I said. "They'll get us over."

He didn't ask unnecessary questions. We worked quickly, ripping hell out of some poor farmer's well-tended vines. When we had twelve of them, I wedged each one halfway through the mesh fence, spacing them evenly from top to bottom.

"Steps," I said.

"But will they hold one's weight?"

"They will if they're counterbalanced. I'll show you."

I stooped down, and Butec clambered up onto my shoulders. He balanced precariously there while I straightened up. "Now," I said, "can you step over the barbed wire and onto the top stake? Don't do it yet, just tell me if you can."

"I can."

"Good." I gripped the top stake on my side of the fence

and put all my weight on it. "Now go ahead," I said.

One of his feet left my shoulders and moved over the wire to the stake. I used all my strength to keep the stake balanced, and then his other foot left my shoulder and cleared the barbed wire.

"Evan?"

"What?"

"Where do I put the other foot?"

"I don't know," I said foolishly. "Can you jump the rest of the way?"

"Perhaps," he said. And, abruptly, he did just that. As soon as his weight left the stake I was leaning on, I rather foolishly sprawled forward against the fence.

Butec landed on the other side in a catlike crouch. His cap dropped off in the course of his descent, and his wig, the adhesive tape loosened by perspiration, was flapping a bit oddly. But he spun around to face me, a triumphant smile on his round white face. "Are you all right, Evan?" he asked.

"Yes, of course," I said. It was I who should have been asking the question—after all, he was the one who had just jumped seven feet to the ground. "And you?"

"Quite well. But now how will you scale the fence?"

I showed him how. It was his turn to lean his weight upon each of the stakes in turn while I climbed them one by one to the top of the fence. When I reached the top, I swung my right leg over and stood with one foot on either side of the highest stake. It was an odd feeling, like that which a child experiences when manipulating a teeter-totter all by himself. I poised to jump, then sprang with both feet at once, just clearing the topmost strand of barbed wire with my left foot. My landing was not precisely catlike. My feet hit the ground, then my hands, and then I did a neat, if unplanned, little somersault and wound up standing on my own two feet. If I'd tried to do just that, I couldn't have managed it in a thousand years, but in spite of myself I'd done a bit of tumbling that Sofija and her band of Latvian gymnasts might have been proud of.

Milan congratulated me warmly. "One can see you have had much practice at this sort of thing, Evan."

"A bit," I said. I had in fact fallen out of a tree in crossing from Italy into Yugoslavia and another time I fell off a train in Czechoslovakia, but this was the first time I'd ever acquitted myself so acrobatically.

"And now?"

"We move the stakes," I said, "and play the same game again to get into Hungary."

Some of the stakes didn't want to move. They were wedged quite tightly into the steel mesh and seemed content to remain there forever. Milan and I wrestled them out one by one and scurried across the wide gravel path with them. On the Hungarian side was another vineyard that looked startlingly like the one we had just passed through except that the vines were set a bit farther apart. It is always jarring to discover that crossing a border does not entail a great change of terrain. One almost expects the ground itself to change color, as on a map, and one has to remind oneself that the ground was there long before there were countries and long before the various portions of the ground had been awarded names and dimensions.

We wedged our stakes into the Hungarian fence. I dropped to my knees, and once again Milan mounted my shoulders. Either he had gained weight in the past few minutes or I was growing weaker; whatever the case, it was not so easy to straighten up this time. But I did, and used one hand to support a stake from beneath, and Butec, cap and wig once again fixed neatly in place, took a little leap and flapped like a bird and landed again like a cat, spinning around at

**70**

once to beam at me with triumph.

"And now you, Evan!"

I readied myself for the climb. This fence was a shade higher than the other, and I wasn't sure whether Butec would be able to reach the higher stakes. I told him to climb with me, he on his side and I on mine, so that our weights would balance one another off. We both stepped onto the bottom stake, and as we stood there I heard in the west the unmistakable sound of an approaching patrol car.

I dropped to the ground so abruptly that Milan was sent sprawling on the other side. "Border patrol," I said. "Get back and out of sight. I'll try to bluff my way through. If I don't manage it, work your way through to Budapest. Go to a man named Ferenc Mihalyi. Mention my name, tell him as much as you have to. He can arrange passage to the West. He——"

"But my manuscript, Evan!"

"I'll try to get it through. If I fail, you can re-create it in London or America. But hurry!"

The patrol vehicle was already in sight. It resembled a jeep of World War II vintage. One man bent over the wheel. The other knelt on the seat with the barrel of his rifle resting on the top of the windshield. The rifle was pointed at me.

I stepped quickly away from the fence and moved toward the middle of the road. I threw my arms high in the air and began waving them about frantically in a sort of hectic semaphore. The jeep approached and pulled to a stop a few yards from me. The rifle remained trained upon me. The driver swung his lean body out of the jeep and advanced, pistol drawn. The rifleman hesitated for a moment, then got out of the jeep himself.

They began shouting things like *What are you doing here? Do you not know that it is forbidden? How did you*

71

*scale the fence?* Even if I had had any intelligent answers for these questions, it would have been impossible to give them; as soon as one asked a question the other chimed in with yet another question, and no one waited for me to say anything.

They were badgering me in Hungarian, so I jabbered back at them in Slovenian. Hungarian border guards would be apt to understand Serbo-Croat, but Slovenian, spoken only in the westernmost province of Yugoslavia, was likely to be outside their ken. They would recognize it, I guessed, but would be unable to follow it. They were certainly unable to follow what I gave them, which was a rough approximation in Slovenian of the 1916 Proclamation of the Irish Republic. They listened to a few moments of this and then began putting the same questions to me in horribly accented Serbo-Croat.

I stuck with Slovenian and gave them a few more sentences of Padraic Pearse's magnificent speech. It sounds quite marvelous in Slovenian. I swung my arms more wildly than ever, giving what I hoped was a fairly convincing imitation of a lunatic. If I could succeed in assuring them I was a harmless madman, they might not bother to turn me over to their Yugoslav counterparts but might be content to tuck me back into Yugoslavia on their own account, thus saving themselves some red tape.

In which case I could scoot around through the Rumanian border, then hop into Hungary, and with luck rejoin Milan Butec in Hungary. Evidently he had made good his escape. The two Hungarians were paying all their attention to me and hadn't so much as glanced through the fence.

I kept talking, feverishly, earnestly, arms high in the air. The one who had been driving sighed heavily and holstered his pistol. The other lowered his rifle.

And, a few yards to my right, Hungarian words rang in the air.

"Drop your guns, fools! Hands in the air or you die like dogs! You are covered. Quickly!"

The driver's arms shot over his head as if yanked by invisible wires. The rifle slipped from the other guard's hands and clattered upon the gravel. He too held his hands high overhead.

"Get their guns, Evan." This in Slovenian, incredibly.

I scooped up the rifle, then snatched the pistol from the driver's holster. I backed off a few paces and turned to see the shining round face of Milan Butec. He was crouching at the side of the fence, bravely covering two terrified guards with one of our wooden stakes.

"Turn around," I told the pair in Hungarian. They did, and I marched them back to their jeep. I gripped the pistol by the barrel and tapped them each in turn, not too hard, at the base of the skull. They went out like snuffed candles.

The key was in the ignition. I started the jeep and drove it to the side of the fence where our stakes formed a ladder. By standing on the hood of the vehicle, it was a simple matter to climb the rest of the way over the fence and drop safely into Hungary. No acrobatic roll this time, though; I landed on my feet, lost my balance, and landed flat on my behind.

"Are you all right, Evan?"

"I think so," I said. I took his hand, and he helped me up. His wig had loosened up again, and his cap was tilted at a rakish angle, but he did not look foolish at all. He was still holding the silly wooden stake. He followed my eyes to it and smiled shyly. "An old Partisan technique," he said. "The Nazis had all the guns, you see, but we of the Resistance had all the intelligence. And brains will get you guns,

73

but guns will never get you brains. I could not leave you, Evan. How would I ever find Budapest myself? And what was that nonsense you were spouting in Slovenian? Something about Ireland?"

"The Proclamation of the Irish Republic."

"One does not often hear it rendered into that tongue." The two of us began removing the remaining stakes from the fence. "Was it necessary to kill them, Evan?"

"No. They are alive. They'll wake up within the hour."

"Is it safe to leave them alive?"

"I think it's safer than killing them. Their memories should be rather hazy when they come to. And they won't want to have to explain what happened to them. Easier for them all around if they simply forget to report the incident. But if we put a couple of bullets into them, someone else will discover them, and then the alarm will go out."

"I would prefer not to kill them," he said thoughtfully. "One gets tired of killing. You left them the rifle?"

"Yes."

"Perhaps you ought to leave the pistol as well. So the young man will not have to report the loss of his weapon."

"It might be handy to have."

"Perhaps."

I thought it over. All in all, I decided, a pistol could do more harm than good. It was easier to avoid trouble than to shoot one's way out of it. And the simpler we left things for the two border guards, the easier it would be for them to forget the incident. Since 1956 the Hungarians have grown quite accustomed to the periodic escape of part of the citizenry. Two more men crossing the border would be easily ignored if we did everything possible to facilitate it.

I engaged the safety catch and tossed the pistol over the fence. It landed just a few feet from the form of its unconscious owner.

"Good," Milan Butec said. "Weapons make me nervous."

"Wooden stakes are safer, eh?"

"Undoubtedly. And, of course, should one encounter a vampire, they are more effective than guns, are they not?"

"They are."

"Simple peasants that we are, we must of course believe in vampires."

"And werewolves, too."

"To be sure."

And like simple peasants, we trudged on through the vineyard north into Hungary.

# 8

---

In the late afternoon, clouds covered the sun, and the air turned cold. We had walked a few miles cross-country after entering Hungary, then switched to the roads. We were never on the road for more than a quarter of an hour before someone would stop and give us a ride, but the rides were invariably in farmers' wagons and rarely carried us more than three or four miles at a clip. It was slow going, and I could see that it was getting to Butec. He didn't complain—indeed, most of the time he said nothing at all—but I knew he was tiring.

I hoped he could hold out until we reached Debrecen, the chief city of Hajdu Province in the northeast. There was a man named Sandor Kodaly in Debrecen who knew of me and whom I could trust. I was fairly sure he could provide shelter for the night and either he or friends of his could ease our way across the border into Czechoslovakia. Fence-climbing left one with a sense of accomplishment, but it was also damned dangerous, and I didn't want to push our luck any more than I had to.

But by nightfall we were no further than Komadi, a good forty miles short of Debrecen. Had I been by myself, I might have pushed on, but Milan Butec was an old man who, after the day's efforts, had every right in the world to be a tired old man. He was walking more slowly now and with visible effort. And yet he had not offered a word of complaint.

"We will not go any further," I told him. We had taken to speaking Hungarian to one another to get ourselves in the habit. His Hungarian was rather heavily accented but otherwise sound. He had told me that he could speak passable Czech as well, which might or might not be helpful; we would be crossing through Slovakia, where they speak a very different tongue from the language spoken in the western sectors of Bohemia and Moravia. Once we entered Poland, he had added, I would have to do the talking for both of us. He spoke no Polish, no Lithuanian, and no Lettish. He could read and write Russian but was unable to converse in it.

"We will stop here for the night," I explained. "Here in Komadi. Tomorrow we can continue to Debrecen and find friends who will help us across the border."

"We could push on tonight if you wish."

"Tomorrow is time enough."

"I know that I am slowing you down, Evan."

"There is no hurry," I said. And, I thought, that was true enough. The faster we moved, the sooner we would get to Latvia. And the sooner we got to Latvia, the sooner we would find ourselves unable to rescue Sofija, and would thus have to turn around and head for home. I was in no hurry to get back to New York. There was a pudgy little

**78**

man who had a habit of turning up there with undesired assignments, and I was in no rush to see him for some time.

"I am beginning to tire, Evan."

"So am I."

"Is there a hotel in Komadi?"

"Hotels are dangerous," I said. "They want to see one's papers and we haven't any. Guest houses are as bad. I think we'd do better to cross through the town and put up at a farmhouse to the north."

"Do the farmers take in guests?"

"We shall see."

The first farmer we approached was gracious enough but explained he had no room for us. But he had a cousin just a quarter mile down the road who, he assured us, would make us welcome. Just a few pengo and we would be given comfortable beds, a hearty dinner, and a good country breakfast in the morning.

The cousin, it turned out, was a young widow with black eyes and hair and milk-white skin. She had been in the country eleven years, having moved there just before the birth of her one child, a daughter with the same plain good looks as the mother.

"We were in Budapest," she told us after dinner. "My husband and I, we were married almost a year. I was from this part of the country and went to Budapest to the University, and met Armin and married him, and after the Revolution he was taken with the others and put up against the wall and executed. And so I did not care to remain in Budapest any longer. Will you have more coffee?"

Dinner was a thick veal stew on a bed of light noodles, all highly spiced and very filling. Milan made an effort to stay awake after dinner but was not quite equal to the task. Our hostess showed him to his room. I suspect he fell asleep on the way to the bed.

The daughter went to sleep shortly thereafter. Eva—I never learned her last name—sat with me in the living room before the fireplace. When the fire burned down, I went outside for more wood. I returned with the wood, and she appeared from the kitchen with a bottle of Tokay. We drank a few glasses. She talked of art and literature and the cinema. There were few persons with whom one could discuss such subjects in the country, she told me. She missed Budapest, with its busy coffee houses and its bubbling culture. But she did not miss the political hubbub of the city or the memories of 1956.

"It is lonely here," she said. "But people are good, and I have much family in the area. This was my own father's house, I am used to it, it comforts me. But one grows lonely."

"You will marry again."

"Perhaps. I have been ten years widowed. Sometimes a man comes to help me work the farm for a season and stays with me for a season. There have been those who would have stayed longer, but I was married to a fine and intelligent man, and when one is used to gold, one does not care for silver."

I said nothing.

"Married at twenty and widowed at twenty-one, and now I am thirty-two and alone in the world. There is but a little wine left in the bottle. Shall we finish it?"

We finished it. The drink had brought a flush to her white cheeks, and she was breathing a bit heavily as she got to her feet. "And now it is time for me to show you to your room, Evan."

She walked unsteadily before me. I thought of Annalya in Macedonia. Macedonia was many miles away.

The room was small, furnished simply with a narrow bed, a chest of drawers, a single chair, and a cast-iron woodburning stove. She lit a fire in the stove, and it warmed the room. She came toward me, her dark eyes shining, her black hair hanging loose and free.

"Eva and Evan," she said.

Her mouth tasted of sweet wine. She sighed urgently and pressed tight against me. Her arms went around me, tightened. Her hands moved over my back, and her mouth kissed greedily. I was very pleased that we had been unable to reach Debrecen and that the first farmhouse had had no room for us. "Eva and Evan," she said again, and I kissed her again, and her slim, sweet body was warm to my touch.

We undressed in the glow of the woodburning stove. I took off my jacket and my sweaters and my shirt and my trousers and my underwear, and I looked at her as she slipped out of her clothing and I saw the odd look in her eyes and I looked down at myself and saw all those silly little oilcloth packets taped to various portions of my anatomy.

"What——"

"A book," I said.

"You have written a book?"

"No. I am a . . . a courier. I am taking the book to the West." I hesitated. "It is a political book."

"Ah," she said. She sighed. "I should have known you were a political man. I am always attracted to political men, and of course they are the most dangerous men for women to love." She looked at me again and suddenly she began to giggle. "You look very silly," she said.

And then we were both laughing. She threw herself into my arms, and her hands touched the oilskin packet strapped to my back, and she began to laugh again, and her thighs pressed against the packets taped round my thighs, and her breasts pushed against the packet taped to my chest, and she kept kissing and giggling and kissing and laughing until we tumbled gently into bed. Her hand reached for me and found me, and she said, "Thank God it's not a longer book, we wouldn't want anything taped *here,*" and, while this was the funniest thing she had said all night, neither of us laughed or giggled or in fact said anything at all until, in the throes of sweet, desperate passion, she cried out with love and raked my oilskin packet with her nails.

# 9

----------------------------------------------------------------

Butec slept for twelve hours, just twice as long as he had assured me was his usual custom. I didn't attempt to wake him. He would travel better for being well rested, and I myself was in no great hurry to move on. While Eva slept I sat in the kitchen drinking coffee and reading a rather excessively heroic biography of Lajos Kossuth, Hungary's national hero who led the Revolution of 1848. The book was back on the shelf, and I was back in bed by the time Eva awoke. She made little mewing and purring sounds and came to me, soft and sweet and sleep-warm. After an hour or so she padded contentedly from the bedroom and went to cook breakfast.

I did a few helpful things, chopped a basket of firewood with a heavy double-bitted axe, brought up a bucket of water from the pump, built up the fire on the hearth. Eva's daughter breakfasted with us, then hurried off to the road to wait for the school bus.

"Every day she goes to school," Eva said, "and every night I have to teach her that almost everything they have taught her is untrue. But she is bright and learns quickly to separate the true from the false. It would be easier, though, if I could keep her out of school and educate her at home. The law does not permit this, however."

We talked of music and literature and politics, and we talked not at all of the pleasure we had given one another in that narrow bed. I thought of my son, Todor, and I wondered idly if I might have gifted Eva with a permanent souvenir of our night of love.

A disquieting thought, that. I was not entirely pleased with the image of myself as a happy wanderer contributing to the global population explosion by leaving a trail of precious bastards in my wake. Yet not entirely displeased, either—children are rather good things to have and no less enjoyable simply because one doesn't have them underfoot all the time.

I mused over this, and it must have shown in my face because Eva asked me what I was thinking about. "Only that you are very lovely," I said, at which she blushed furiously and found something to do in another room.

Butec emerged, dressed and fresh-looking, not long after. While Eva fed him I returned to my room and scribbled a brief note in Hungarian: *In the unlikely event that our love bears fruit*, I wrote, *I should like to know of it. You may always reach me through Ferenc Mihalyi*. I added his Budapest address and left the note where she would certainly find it.

By noon we were on our way to Debrecen.

Sandor Kodaly had the body of a wrestler and the face

of a medieval philosopher, with long, flowing hair, deep-set eyes, and finely chiseled features. He was in his early fifties, a widower with three unmarried sons. He and his sons ran a sizable farm outside Debrecen and made it prosper in spite of the frequent annoyance of five-year plans and new economic policies. I had never met him before, yet everything about him and his household was instantly familiar, an extraordinary incidence of *déjà vu*. It took me a few minutes to figure it out, and then I realized what it was. He and his sons and his farm were a Central European version of the Cartwright family, the *Bonanza* television program translated into Hungarian.

"So you are Evan Tanner," he said. "And your companion is——"

"A man with temporary amnesia," I said. "He has forgotten his name, and so, for that matter, have I."

"Ah." Kodaly nodded wisely. "That is sensible enough. There are times when men do well to be nameless. No man can reveal what he does not know, is it not so? And I cannot easily betray your companion without knowing who he is."

"I do not fear betrayal at your hands."

"Why not?"

"Because I trust you."

"Oh? That may be foolish. I, on the other hand, am not that much a fool. I do not trust you."

Milan, on my right, remained heroically calm. So did I, though perhaps less heroically. There was nothing I could think of to say, so I waited for Kodaly to explain.

"What you require," he said, "is simple enough. Entry to Czechoslovakia across the eastern frontier. No problem at all. I have business and personal interests that necessitate my crossing that particular border at will. Thus it is well within my power to assist you. The question is"—he paused dramatically—"whether it is in my *interest*."

"How do you mean?"

He got to his feet. "There are some points I must be certain of. You say that you are Evan Tanner, but Evan Tanner I know only through correspondence. From what I know through this correspondence, Evan Tanner, is on the side of the angels. But I would prefer a bit more assurance—that you are truly you and that you are a man I would wish to help. Who in my country knows you? Who has met you face to face and would be able to identify you? Who, that is, who would also be a man I know and can rely upon?"

"There is a young man in Budapest named Ferenc Mihalyi. He knows me. As a matter of fact, he helped me across the southern border once."

"Is that so?" He turned to the doorway. "Erno!" His youngest son, as tall as his father but slim as a reed, stepped quickly into the room. "You know Ferenc Mihalyi in Budapest, do you not? Study this man here, the younger one. Fix his face in your mind. Then go to Budapest and ask Mihalyi if this man is Evan Tanner and what he knows of Evan Tanner."

Erno fixed clear blue eyes on me. I had the feeling that I was having my picture taken, that after ten seconds he would open his mouth to dispense a perfect Polaroid photograph of me. I, in turn, studied him, while Milan Butec fidgeted quietly at my side.

"You have a phrase or two that might help identify you to Mihalyi?"

I thought for a moment. "Yes," I said. "You might tell him that the man who was not my uncle is presently burning in Hell."

"He will understand what this means?"

"Yes, and he'll be glad to know it." The last time I had seen Ferenc, he had helped me smuggle a Slovak Nazi to safety, a task he had not at all relished. He would be pleased to know that my nonuncle had joined his ancestors.

"Repeat, please."

I did.

"Erno, repeat what this man has said and fix it in your memory."

Erno got the message right, word for word, and asked his father if that would be all. It would, Kodaly said, and he should now drive to Budapest and return as speedily as possible.

Erno left us. Milan asked me, in Slovenian, how long it would be before we could get away from these crazy people. I told him I had no idea. Could I speed the process? I told him I doubted it.

"Tanner? While Erno goes to Budapest, you and your companion are my guests. In a sense you are my prisoners as well. My sons and I are armed, you see. It would be unwise of you to attempt to leave this house."

"I had no such intention."

"Very good. Meanwhile, there is food, there is drink, there are beds if you are tired. Books if you wish to read. Do you play chess? Or your friend?"

I play but not very well. Milan said that he played, and Kodaly asked if he would care to have a game. I watched with savage delight while Milan beat him six games straight.

Erno Kodaly had a fast car that he evidently enjoyed driving at an excessive rate of speed. He was back in time for dinner, he had seen Ferenc, and all was well.

"This man is definitely Evan Tanner," he reported to his father, "and Evan Tanner is definitely to be trusted and assisted."

"I thought as much," Kodaly said. He turned to me. "Of course you will not hold against me the fact that I am by nature a cautious man."

**87**

"Certainly not."

"Then let us have dinner, and in an hour's time you will be in Czechoslovakia."

"Papa, there's more." Erno approached me. "Ferenc introduced me to another man who said that he knew you, that you had met. His name is Lajos." I remembered a tall man with a broad forehead and a neatly trimmed gray moustache, an official in the Ministry of Transportation and Communication. "Lajos told me to give you this," he added, handing me a thick manila folder. "He said that you might know what it is and what to do with it."

I took the folder, mystified. I opened it. It was crammed full of a variety of official-looking documents. I leafed through them. They were all in Chinese.

"These are Chinese," I said cleverly.

"That is what Lajos suspected."

"Well, score one for Lajos. What are they?"

"He does not know."

"Where did he get them? And when?"

"He did not say. He thought perhaps you could read them. He thought perhaps they might be important."

"They might be very important," I said. "Or they might be old laundry tickets."

"Pardon me?"

"Nothing." I can speak enough Chinese to know when I'm being insulted by a waiter or a laundryman but not much more than that. And I've never taken the time to learn to read it. I've always had the feeling that no one can really read Chinese, not even the Chinese people themselves. I waded through this miasma of documents and wondered just how Lajos had acquired this particular albatross and why he had felt compelled to drape it around my particular neck.

I wanted to chuck the whole mess into the fireplace, but that wouldn't do. It might be important. Things do tend to

88

happen for a reason, and evidently one of my hitherto un-
suspected roles in the game of life was to carry this little
bundle of chicken tracks from Point A to Point B.

And I had wanted to travel light...

"Can you read it, Mr. Tanner?"

"No."

"Is it important?"

"I don't know."

"What will you do with it all?"

"I don't know that either." I hefted the file. "There's so
damned much of it." I got to my feet. "You'll have to help
me, Milan. Sandor, is there a room we can use for a few
moments? And I will need a scissors and a few yards of
oilcloth."

An hour or so later we crossed the border into Czechoslovakia in the false bottom of a half-ton panel truck. I had
never before known that panel trucks could have false bot-
toms. Suitcases, yes. But panel trucks?

This one—Kodaly's own—did. It was a sort of panlike
arrangement that fitted between the bottom of the trunk
compartment (or whatever the hell they call that part of the
trunk where you put things) and the axles and such below.
It was not quite as deep as a coffin and considerably less
comfortable. In it Milan Butec and I rode in silence. There
was no point in talking—one couldn't hear anything but
the road noise, which was quite deafening. There wasn't
enough room to breathe deeply or enough air to make it
worthwhile anyway. There was no room to move around,
or to scratch oneself, or to do much of anything, really, but
lie there and wait for the interminable ride to terminate. The
truck started, the truck stopped, the truck started, the truck
stopped, the truck started, the truck stopped, and finally
Sandor Kodaly let us out of that horrible dark hole.

I got out at once and did all the things I had been unable to do—yawned, took deep breaths, jumped around, scratched myself, and otherwise assured myself that I was still able to move. I looked for Milan and saw that he was still lying there in the false bottom of the truck. For a horrible moment I thought he had quietly and uncomplainingly died, but then I realized that he was simply too stiff to move by himself. I helped him out, and he moved very slowly and stiffly, like Robby the Robot, until at last his blood began circulating again and his muscles remembered their proper functions.

I asked Sandor where we were.

"Near Medzilaborce."

I tried to remember where Medzilaborce was. "But that's in the north," I said. "That's just a few miles from the Polish border."

"Perhaps fifteen kilometers."

"I thought you were only taking us across the border."

The fine, sensitive features relaxed in a smile. "So I drive an extra hour here and an extra hour back. I kept you several hours at my house while I checked on you. That was an indignity, albeit a necessary one. But perhaps I can even the tally by helping you a little further along on your journey, you see? Now you do not have all of Czechoslovakia to cross. An hour's walk, and you will be in Poland."

I started to say something, something appropriately grateful, but all at once Milan shouldered me aside and stepped in front of Kodaly.

"You drove us an extra hour," he said.

"It was my pleasure——"

"You left us an extra unnecessary hour in that bouncing, dreary, cramped metal coffin. We were already across the border, we were already in Czechoslovakia, but you left us in there for an hour of bouncing and no breathing and no moving and——"

"It was uncomfortable?" Kodaly seemed honestly puzzled. "I have never been in there, it never occurred to me. It was bad for you in there? And to think, once we crossed the border, you could have been riding in the truck with me. But it never even occurred to me..."

Milan was unable to take any more of this. While I made our apologies and expressed our gratitude to Kodaly, he stalked sullenly down the road toward Poland. He walked stiffly, partly because he was trying to hold his temper in check, partly because his legs were still stiff from the long, cramped ride, and partly, too, because he had little oilcloth packets taped all over him, little packets filled with papers covered with chicken tracks.

I had to run to catch up with him. And it was ten minutes before he could relax enough to speak to me. He was that furious. The idea that anyone could have been so utterly insensitive to his comfort utterly maddened him.

"It's an hour's walk to the border," I told him. "If you wish, we can wait until morning."

"Why would we want to do that?"

"If you're tired——"

"Tired? Angry, yes. Exhausted, yes. Tired I am not."

"Then, you would rather cross the border tonight?"

"As soon as possible, Evan." He heaved a sigh. "I have never been in Czechoslovakia before. I never intend to return. I wish to be out of Czechoslovakia as quickly as possible."

"Actually it's a beautiful country——"

"I do not doubt this for a moment, Evan. But I do not want to *see* it. I want to remember nothing whatsoever of Czechoslovakia but that horrible ride and a quick walk

91

through the darkness. That and nothing more. And with only that unpleasant empty memory to dwell upon, I will thus soon forget the entire incident. And the sooner I forget that horrid ride, the happier I will be. That stupid man! That boor! That damned truck!"

# 10

---

We saw as little of Czechoslovakia as possible. Had we seen any less, we wouldn't have been able to stay on the road. As it was, there was only a thin sliver of moon, and we walked through almost total darkness. The road cut to the east and would have taken us out of our way, so we left it after a mile or so and cut directly north through a sparse forest of scrub pine. We heard some rifle shots off in the distance. Milan was alarmed until I suggested that it was probably just a poacher trying to get himself a deer or roebuck.

The border, when we reached it, was positively anticlimactic. Just a simple fence, perhaps six feet tall, easy to climb, and with no barbed wire at its top. The average farmer protects his fields more thoroughly than Poland and Czechoslovakia bother to guard their common frontier. The customs posts on the roads were probably thorough enough, but anyone who wanted to take the trouble to circumvent them could cross back and forth pretty much at will. Milan and I both climbed up and over and down with ease, and that, really, was all there was to it.

"Now," I said, "we are in Poland."

"Now I can afford the luxury of being tired."

"Are you?"

"A bit, Evan. But let us press on for a time. And, if we are in Poland, should you not talk to me in Polish?"

"I thought you didn't speak it."

"Teach me."

The more languages one knows, the easier it is to add another. We walked through the night, made our way through the woods and onto a road, and followed it in what I hoped was the approximate direction of Krakow. The ancient Polish city lay about a hundred miles to the west and was thus out of our way, but I knew people in Krakow whose assistance would be worth the slight detour. We walked along an empty road and I taught him words and phrases of Polish. He would answer back in a sort of pidgin Polish, working the new words into Serbo-Croat sentences, and then I would put his sentences into true Polish, and he would repeat them again to get them straight in his mind.

I didn't expect that he would retain much of the language this way. But before long he would be able to follow simple conversations and make himself understood without inordinate difficulty. In the meanwhile he told me of his experiences during the war, fighting at the head of one of Tito's small bands of partisans. He talked of ambushes, of traps laid in the night, of no quarter asked and none given. He told me how a Serbian town had looked after a detachment of Ante Pavelic's Ustashi fascists had finished massacring the inhabitants and he told me of the revenge his men had taken upon the Ustashis.

94

"We took a platoon of sixty of them by night, Evan. We garroted the sentries with wire nooses and we murdered the rest of them in their beds. There were only eight of us. We used knives, long knives. One or two awoke, but none had time to cry out. We were very swift, and most of them died sleeping. We killed them all but one.

"And that one, Evan, we left alive. We roused him from his sleep and took him from bed to bed and showed him all of his dead comrades, and we told him why they had been killed and that all Ustashi murderers could expect to die. And then we crushed his hands and feet with rifle butts and we put out his eyes so that he would never be able to recognize us. But we left him alive, Evan, and we left his tongue in his head. You see, we wanted him to be able to tell others what had happened and why. And do you know, after that night, there was a great decrease in Ustashi terror in that sector of Montenegro. A great number of their men deserted."

"And the man with the crushed hands and feet?"

"He still lives, Evan. He is in a sanitarium outside of Zagreb. He is only—let me see—not yet forty, I would say. He was a boy of fifteen when the massacre occurred."

"Fifteen——"

"Fifteen years. A schoolboy. And yet he had murdered Serbian infants and old women. Fifteen years, and my own men and I crippled and blinded him."

He fell silent for a moment or two. Then he said, "I have not talked of that boy for many years. I have tried not to think of him. I know that what we did that night was necessary. It saved lives, it shortened the war, it helped far more persons than the sixty who suffered in it. Yet I cannot forget that boy. It was I myself who put out his eyes, Evan." He held out his hands and looked at them. "I myself. Do you wonder that I hate war, Evan? And governments? And large nations making larger wars?"

"You did what you had to do, Milan."

"In a better world," he said, "I would not have had to do it."

We spent that night in a forest. There was an abundance of fallen half-rotted timber lying about, and I built a small fire in a clearing, and we camped around it. Milan slept while I tended the fire. He got up about the same time the sun did. He yawned and stretched and smiled. "I have not slept on the ground in more than twenty years," he said. "I had forgotten how comfortable it is. Have we any food?"

"No."

"Excuse me. I will be back soon."

I assumed he was off to perform some sort of lavatory function and when he hadn't returned after a quarter of an hour, I was certain he was either in trouble or in very ill health. But he came back beaming with a dead rabbit in one hand and a bloody knife in the other.

"Breakfast," he announced.

The hare was a doe, nice and plump. He skinned it and sectioned it with astonishing skill. We cut a pair of slim branches from a tree and impaled pieces of rabbit meat upon them, then roasted them over our little fire. A sort of *lapin en brochette*, or rabbitkabob. It wasn't the most suitable breakfast in the world, but it was tasty and filling.

I asked Milan how he had caught the hare. He shrugged as if it were the sort of thing any fool ought to be able to accomplish. "I found a place where hares were likely to be," he said, "and I waited until this one appeared and I brained her with a rock. Then I cut her throat and bled her and brought her here."

And later, after we had talked of other things and had quite forgotten the little doe, he said, "The only hard part

96

is hitting them with the stone. You have to drop them on the first cast. The rest is just a matter of moving in silence and keeping one's eyes open."

It took me a moment to realize that he was referring to hares. My first thought was of the Ustashi sentries. Hunting is the same sort of business, I suppose, whatever the quarry.

We were in Krakow by nightfall. We spent most of our time in horse-drawn carts, which was fine with me. I was at least as bored with hiking as Milan was and equally tired of the countryside. I wanted to be in a warm house in a city where I could get a bath and a shave and clean clothes. Our dirty, unshaven faces were a good disguise—we looked entirely too disreputable to be persons of any importance— but mine, at least, was a nuisance. It itched. So, for that matter, did the rest of me, especially under the damned oilcloth packets.

We entered Krakow from the east, passing first through the new city of Nowa Huta. It had all been built up after the war to accommodate workers at the Lenin Metallurgical combine. We passed through streets laid out in neat geometrical monotony, street after street of identical rows of semidetached houses. Little boxes made of ticky-tacky. We might as well have been in Kew Gardens. The twentieth century imposes its own special brand of monotony whenever it's given a free hand, and it doesn't seem to matter whether the government is capitalist or socialist or fascist; either way, the end result is a sort of Levittown of the mind.

After Nowa Huta, clean and fresh and modern and sterile, Krakow was a glorious relief. The city was one of the very few in Poland to remain intact throughout the war. There were no bombings by either side. The population was largely devastated, of course—Oswiecim, which the Germans called Auschwitz, is only thirty miles to the west. But the castles

97

and cathedrals and old buildings remain, and the city is beautiful.

I steered us through the center of the city, into the oldest section around the Jagiellonian University, a center of Polish learning for over six centuries. Copernicus studied there, and later determined that the earth was not the center of the universe. My comrades in the Flat Earth Society are inclined to dispute this and perhaps they are right. What does the movement of stars and planets have to do with the center of the universe? Milan's universe was centered in a Montenegrin town called Savnik. The center of the world for Tadeusz Orlowicz was indisputably Krakow, however frequently he found it advisable to leave it.

And the center of my own universe? I pondered this in silence while we walked through the narrow old streets of the student quarter. There was, I decided, no permanent center to my universe. Sometimes it was a hut in Macedonia, sometimes a cottage in Hungary, sometimes an apartment on West 107th Street. I wondered if it might be important for a man's universe to have a center and if there was any vital self-discovery I could make through the realization that mine did not. Men have told me that they like to sleep every night in the same bed. If I slept, perhaps I would feel this way.

But self-analysis and self-absorption are subtle forms of self-destruction, leading sooner or later to what Hindi call nirvana and psychiatrists call catatonia. The center of the universe, for the moment, was Krakow, and the man at its very hub was Tadeusz Orlowicz. I did not know where he lived—he found it advisable to move frequently, and to keep his address a secret—but I did know where I might be likely to find him, or to get word of him.

We worked our way in and around the university district. In an alley off Wislna Street was a small cafe of which I had often heard in the past. It appeared to be closed, but I had been told that it almost invariably appeared to be closed. I went to the door and rang the bell, one long, two short, two long, three short. Then I waited for approximately three minutes before repeating the process.

An old woman, dressed in loose black clothing, opened the door a crack and peered out at me.

I said, "My friend and I are fond of roasted partridge and understand it is obtainable here."

"It is out of season," the old woman said.

"Some game is always in season."

"One tires of game."

"One cannot afford to tire of the game."

It was an elaborate sequence and, I felt, rather a foolish one. It brought to mind the pudgy man from Washington and cryptic scribbles on Juicy Fruit gum wrappers. And what good did the password do? All the woman could really be sure of, after we'd gone through this silly bit of business, was that if I were a government agent, I was an exceedingly well-informed one and thus most dangerous.

She was not that deep a thinker. She opened the door wider, and I entered with Milan close behind me. She led us through one darkened room and into another. There were half a dozen tables, all of them empty. A candle glowed on one of them at the rear. She pointed us toward that table, and we took seats.

"You wish to eat?"

"Please."

"Chlodnik? Kolduny? Tea?"

"Please."

Chlodnik is a cold beet soup not unlike borscht. Kolduny is dumplings stuffed with ground mutton. Tea is tea. She brought food to us, and we ate.

From time to time a face would peer at us through a

darkened window a few yards away. I had the feeling we were being studied by a variety of persons. Eventually the old woman returned to clear the table. She asked if we wanted anyone.

I took a pencil and wrote out a brief note. "Since there is no partridge," I said, "you might have this given to the sparrow hawk."

Sparrow Hawk was not exactly a code name for Orlowicz; more a nickname. She seemed to know whom I meant and to be unsurprised by the request. She went away and a while later she returned with another pot of tea.

Through all of this Milan had been nicely silent. But by now I suspect he was getting echoes of the bit of idiocy we'd undergone in Hungary. He said softly in Serbo-Croat, "If we are bundled again into the underpart of some slimy trunk——"

"Do not worry," I said in Polish.

"I am not worried, I am simply determined. At this very moment there are guns trained on us. Did you know that?"

"No, but I'm not surprised."

"Nor am I. In their place I would do the same. Still, it is tiresome. I have told you how guns play upon my nerves. From where I am sitting, I can see a blackened gun barrel at the mouth of a knothole in the wall behind you. Do not turn, the idiot might shoot. I wish I were in Savnik."

We nursed that pot of tepid tea for three quarters of an hour. Then the woman came out and led us into yet another back room and down a flight of stairs to a dank basement. There she turned us over to a very young man wearing a very false beard. "You will come with me," he said, and an accurate prediction it was, for we did.

He led us through a maze of subterranean tunnels that led me to conclude that the word "underground," in Krakow, was taken very literally. We emerged either half a mile away or right back where we started—it was impossible to guess, with all the twists and turns the tunnels had taken. We went up a short flight of steps, down a hallway, up two more flights of steps, and paused in front of a door upon which our false-bearded escort duly knocked.

The door opened, and there was Tadeusz.

In good, clear American he said, "Evan, you son of a bitch, it's really you, isn't it?" and pulled me inside, and motioned Milan in after me, and nodded reassuringly to our escort, and closed the door, and punched playfully at my shoulder, and without further preliminaries filled three small glasses with clear Polish vodka.

"To Poland," he said, "citadel of culture, home of Chopin and Paderewski and Copernicus, land of beautiful lakes and forests, and to all the stupid Polacks all over the world, long may they wave."

We drank.

He was a most unusual man. He was, in appearance, the sort of tall, gaunt, blond, dreamy-eyed young Pole who plays upon the piano in a Swiss mountain resort while quietly dying of tuberculosis. Appearances could hardly be more deceiving. I had met him in New York, where he appeared occasionally on fund-raising and propaganda missions that took him to Polish communities throughout the world. For three weeks he lived in my apartment, sleeping in my bed, sometimes alone, more often with any of several Negro and Puerto Rican girls with whom he would fall hopelessly in love for two or three days, after which time his love would burn out and the girls would return to the streets from whence they had come.

He was a fervent Polish Nationalist who despised the overwhelming majority of his countrymen. He was a Christian who hated churches and clergymen, a Socialist who loathed Russia and China, a devout Pacifist with an astonishing capacity for ruthless violence. He smoked several packs of cigarettes a day, drank enormous quantities of vodka, and fornicated whenever given the opportunity.

He said, "Evan, how many Polacks does it take to change a light bulb? Five—one to hold the bulb and four to turn the ladder. Evan, how do you tell the groom at a Polish wedding? He's the one in the clean bowling shirt. Evan, how do you keep a Polish girl from screwing? Marry her!"

He roared, I laughed, and Milan stood around looking politely puzzled. Tadeusz told half a dozen more Polish jokes, then came abruptly to a halt. "But you have been traveling and need refreshment. Are you hungry?"

"We ate at the cafe. But we need to bathe and shave, and I will also need fresh clothing for both of us and a roll of adhesive tape."

"Of course," Tadeusz said.


After the bath and the shave, after I'd used fresh tape to affix the silly packets once again to various portions of myself, after I had dressed again in clean clothing, I felt, if not like a new man, at least like a much-improved version of the old one. While Milan bathed I sat in the front room with Tadeusz and we talked about friends in America.

"So," he said at length, "you have come to Krakow. Business in Poland, or is this merely a way station?"

"Precisely that."

"You will want transportation, eh? Where do you go next? West Germany, perhaps?"

"No. Lithuania."

His eyebrows shot up. "You are taking Milan Butec to Lithuania?"

"How . . . how——"

"Evan, please. Even a dumb Polack can count past ten without taking off his shoes. I know the man has left

Yugoslavia. I know what he looks like. I know a wig when I see one, especially so crude a wig. It's as obvious as the beard on that young moron who fetched you here. You don't have to worry about me. Why, he was one of my boyhood heroes! And I respect him now more than ever. But Lithuania! Polacks are stupid enough, but you would take him among the crazy Litvaks?"

He poured another vodka while I gave him the briefest possible explanation of my trip to Latvia. Tadeusz, as it happened, was just the right sort of person for this story. It made perfect sense to him that someone would go to all this trouble just to reunite two lovers. Politics was politics, and a good cigar was a smoke, but love, after all, made the world go round. His words, not mine.

He drank his vodka down, lit a fresh cigarette from the butt of the old, flipped the old into the fireplace, poured himself more vodka, and sighed the languid sigh of the tubercular pianist he wasn't.

"I understand and sympathize," he assured me. "But."

"But what?"

"But it would suit my avowedly selfish purposes more if you were going directly to the West."

"It is difficult to enter Lithuania?"

"No, that I can readily arrange. And in return, if you please, you will do me a favor. A great favor."

"What?"

He dug his hands into his jacket pockets. He drew them out again, and in each hand he held a flat black cylinder about half an inch thick and three inches in diameter.

"Two of them," he said. "One for New York, one for Chicago. Microfilm. Vital that it gets there. You know the people and you know how to get around. I'll get you to Lithuania, you'll get this crud back to the States. Fair enough?"

At which point Milan emerged from the bathroom, nattily dressed, neatly shaved, with his wig on backward.

I sat down and started to cry.

# 11

-----------------------------------------------------------------

"If nothing else," Tadeusz had said, "this government of
ours makes the trains run on time." The same left-handed
compliment had been paid to Mussolini's regime in Italy,
where it may or may not have been true. It was indisputably
true in Poland. After a little more than twenty-four hours
in Krakow, during which time we toured Wawel Castle,
walked the banks of the Vistula, and roamed extensively
through the old quarter, during which time Milan caught up
on his sleep and I sidestepped Tadeusz's constant offers of
feminine companionship, and during which time identity
cards were carefully prepared for us and routes arranged—
after this fruitful and pleasant twenty-four hours of rest and
relaxation we boarded a night train for Warsaw. The con-
ductor looked in on us, examined our tickets, mutilated them
professionally with a ticket-punch, examined our identity
cards, returned them unmutilated, and then left us happily

alone in our compartment. Milan went immediately to sleep. I had acquired a handful of paperbound books from Tadeusz, all of them safely apolitical, and I settled myself in my seat and set about reading them.

My name, according to the folding leatherette-bound card I carried, was Casimir Miodowa. Milan had been rechristened Jozef Slowacki. The cards would pass all but the most rigorous sort of inspection and, Tadeusz assured me, ought to get us over the border into the Lithuanian S. S. R. with no difficulty whatsoever.

We looked less like peasants now and more like minor business or government functionaries of one sort or another. We wore suits, crudely tailored but new and clean, with neatly knotted neckties. We carried small suitcases containing only clothing and personal articles, suitcases that could be opened for inspection without the slightest risk of their disclosing anything compromising, suitcases that I intended to discard forever once we were across the frontier. In the meantime they helped establish our role as middle-class members of the Polish classless society.

I read, Milan slept. Our train reached Warsaw on schedule. I roused Milan, and we changed for another train to Bialystok in the northeast. There we changed trains a second time, cutting north and west to Gizycko near the border. It was morning when we left the train, and Gizycko, at the edge of the Masurian lake district, was glorious in the sunshine. Sailboats swept gracefully across Lake Mamry. The water was startlingly blue, the dense woods surrounding the lake a deep and abiding green. We boarded a bus for the frontier. There armed Border Guards had us dismount from the bus, pawed through our luggage, examined our identity cards, noted our names and other particulars, asked us where we were going, how long we would be staying, the nature of our business — in short, made perfect nuisances of themselves by doing ther jobs quite properly. I supplied all the appropriate answers, Milan pointed to his mouth and conveyed to them the notion that he was a mute, and we, like all the other Lithuania-bound passengers, were permitted to return to the bus and cross into Lithuania.

I had thus brilliantly smuggled into the Soviet Union a subversive manuscript, its subversive Yugoslav author, an array of undecipherable Chinese documents, and two spools of microfilm containing plans and information for Polish exile groups in the United States. The microfilm currently reposed in two hollowed-out heels that a friend of Tadeusz's had fastened onto my shoes. Tadeusz had been very enthusiastic about this maneuver, as though he were the first person ever to hit upon the notion of smuggling contraband in a bootheel. I couldn't share his delight; from what I knew of smuggling and customs searches, the bootheel is one of the first places checked.

But it didn't matter. Once they picked me up, the game was over. There was no part of me they could search without finding something incriminating. And here I was, with all of this extremely dangerous contraband, not sneaking *out* of Russia, which would have made a certain amount of sense, but smuggling everything *in*.

It wasn't quite like carrying coals to Newcastle. More, I thought, like leading Christians carefully through the catacombs and emerging on center stage at the Coliseum, just in time for the lion number.

The bus went to Vilna, capital city of the Lithuanian Soviet Socialist Republic. Milan and I went, in another bus, to Kaunas, the old capital city of independent Lithuania from 1919 to 1938, during which time Vilna was a part of Poland. Borders and boundaries change and shift even more rapidly than nations form new teams for new wars. As far as I was concerned, Kaunas, with a population of a quarter of a million, was still the true capital of Lithuania. And the people I knew in Lithuania were the sort who felt the same, and who lived there.

I would have wanted to stop in Kaunas anyway, if only to meet in person some comrades from the Crusade for a Free Lithuania. But there were practical reasons as well. Within a day or so someone processing border records would discover that Casimir Miodowa and Jozef Slowacki did not in fact exist, and at that point it would not be wise for us to be a pair of petit bourgeois Poles. We would need another change of clothing, a transformation from Polish to Soviet citizenship.

Kaunas was mostly postwar construction, a great deal of concrete block houses and shops and factories. All three of the Baltic States had been devastated in World War I, built themselves up slowly but surely in the period between the wars, then served once again as a Russo-German battleground during the second war. Kaunas had been pretty thoroughly demolished in the course of all this warfare. It had been built up again, larger than ever, but there wasn't much of the old city left underneath it all.

I blundered around, asking directions in rusty Lithuanian until we found our way to the right house. I had only one real contact in Lithuania, an old woman named Hescha Uldansa. I had no contacts at all inside Latvia. The Baltic exile groups are forced to operate almost entirely in exile, as the Russian government has an unhappy habit of resettling native sympathizers in Azerbaijan and Kazakhstan, where they aren't likely to function effectively as activists.

So we called on Hescha, a gnarled woman with wens under her eyes and liver spots on her hands and a cracked voice that sounded as though someone had poured a tablespoon of Drano down her larynx.

"So good to see you," she said. "Come in, come in. Tanir, eh? Come inside, shut the door. When we are free again, then we will not have this cold Russian weather, eh?"

We chatted amiably about mutual friends in New York. While she went off to make tea Milan asked in an undertone if we could really understand one another. "Is it really a language? It doesn't sound like anything."

"It sounds a good deal like Lettish."

"Then Lettish doesn't sound like anything, either."

"They both sound quite a bit like Sanskrit."

"Oh, please!"

"It's true," I told him. "They're probably the two oldest Indo-European languages. Don't even try to follow conversations. They'll only give you a headache."

"They already have."

Hescna returned with glasses of tea and little cakes frosted with orange icing. The tea was very good, the cakes were not.

"You speak well," she told me. "But if you will excuse me, I must say that you have lost some of your Lithuanian way of speaking in America." She evidently assumed I had been born in Lithuania, and there was no point in reorienting her. "You speak," she said, "with a distinct Lettish accent."

"I do?"

"It is noticeable, yes."

"I have been associating with Letts in America."

"Well, they are good people, of course. It is unfortunate, though, that their language is a corruption of the pure Lithuanian."

The Letts feel that Lithuanian is a corruption of the pure Lettish. We talked some more, and I told her we would require a change of clothing. I didn't bother saying anything about identity cards. Hescha was a sympathizer, not a conspirator, and a bit senile in the bargain. The less she knew

**109**

about our destination, the better off we were. And it was highly unlikely she would have the sort of connections able to provide false papers or passports.

She brought us clothing, good farmers' clothing, including a fine pair of boots for me that I couldn't possibly wear. They matched the rest of my clothes far better than the Polish business shoes, but to give up my Polish shoes would be to abandon the damned spools of microfilm in the heels. I scuffed up the shoes so that they didn't jar too obviously with the rest of my costume. They would have to do.

"Tanir," she said. "I have a thing to show you, you will be most excited. No one in America knows, I have told no one. Your friend, he is not Lithuanian, no?"

I agreed that Milan was not Lithuanian.

"Then, he can wait here. We will not be long, he would not be interested. But you I show. It is all right?"

I translated the gist of this for Milan. He did not at all mind the thought of being abandoned to silence for a time. The unfamiliar Lithuanian was ringing in his ears.

We walked several blocks. Hescha's carefree manner changed markedly on the way; the little old woman, her shawl pulled tightly around her, looked over her shoulder and peered around corners so busily that I was afraid her excess of precautions would inevitably draw attention to us. Fortunately we reached our destination before this happened. She led me into a doorway, then down a long flight of unlit stairs, then pushed a metal barrel aside to reveal a hidden door. She opened the door with a small key, stepped quickly through, and drew me in behind her. Then, swiftly, she closed and bolted the door.

Inside the windowless room, illuminated by a solitary kerosene lantern, sitting up straight in a tiny narrow bed, was as beautiful a child as I had ever seen in my life.

The little girl regarded us solemnly. Hescha said, "Minna,

this is Mr. Evanis Tanir from America. Tanir, this is Minna."

Minna and I said hello to each other.

"You know who she is?" Hescha whispered furiously.

"Of course not."

"A direct descendant of Mindaugas! A provable descendant! Provable!"

"Mindaugas——"

"The only true king of Lithuania. Over seven hundred years ago Mindaugas died, and never since that day has Lithuania had a monarch upon the throne. False kings thrust upon us by the Poles, yes. But never a king of Lithuania."

There was a Mindaugas who died in 1263. And it was conceivable, I suppose, that this golden-haired angel of a child could be a direct descendant of his. I wasn't especially inclined to believe it, but it was possible. I didn't see what difference it made.

"Minna," the old woman said, "is a very important person. You understand?"

"Why?"

Hescha looked at me as though I had gone suddenly mad. "But you must see! When the Lithuanian monarchy is restored, who will become undisputed Queen of Lithuania?"

"Zsa Zsa Gabor," I said.

"Pardon?"

"Nothing," I said. When the Lithuanian monarchy was restored, I thought privately, rivers would flow upstream, shrimps would whistle, and the First Law of Thermodynamics would be repealed by Act of Congress. The possibility of Lithuania regaining its independence was too remote to take very seriously (the fact that I prefer to take it seriously notwithstanding), but the idea of the restoration of the Mindaugas line after seven centuries...

The mind boggled.

"And so we must keep her here, my sister and I. My

sister stays with Minna during the nights, but during the days she works, and I come here when I can. And Minna must remain in this room, hidden from the Soviet authorities, and——"

"Wait a moment," I said. "She never leaves this room?"

"Of course not."

"She sits in that bed, in this clammy room, and——"

"It is a comfortable room. A soft bed."

"She never goes to school? She never plays with other children? She never gets out in the fresh air?"

"It is too dangerous."

"But——"

"The authorities know of Minna's existence," Hescha said patiently. "If they found her, they would have to remove her as a threat to Soviet unity. They know she will someday be a rallying point for Lithuania. And if she were taken by them, she would be sent far from here, far from her own people. She would be brought up as a Russian, she would forget her Lithuanian heritage. Or she might even be killed——"

"That's ridiculous."

"Can you be certain? Would you have us take chances with the life of such a one?"

"But she must *hate* it here," I said.

"She is content. Minna is a patient child, with the blood of royalty in her veins."

"She must be lonely."

"She sees me. And my sister."

"But children her own age——"

"It is too dangerous, Tanir."

I walked away from Hescha, who was still babbling, and knelt at the side of Minna's bed. She fastened clear blue eyes upon me. Her hair was like spun gold, neatly braided and trailing all the way down her back. Her complexion, despite the dank cellar in which she spent twenty-four impossible hours a day, was still fresh and rosy.

I said, "Hello, Minna."

"Hello, Mr. Tanner."

"Call me Evan, Minna."

"Evan."

What did one say to a child. "How old are you, Minna?"

"Six years. Seven in March."

"Are you happy here?"

"Happy?" As if she did not wholly understand the concept. "I have books to read. Hescha is teaching me how to read. And dolls to play with. Happy?"

Hescha was still carrying on. I ignored her. I said, "Minna, how would you like to go on a long journey? How would you like to come with me to America?"

"America?" She thought about this. "But I am not allowed to go outdoors," she said. She sounded like all the little boys who try to run away from home but aren't allowed to cross streets. "I have to stay in this room forever," she said seriously.

"If you come with me, you will not have to stay inside."

"Is there sun in America? And snow and rain?"

"Yes."

"And are there other children in America? And do children play games and go swimming and go to school? And are there dogs and cats and sheep and goats and pigs there? And lions and tigers?" She motioned toward an orderly pile of books. "In my books there are all such things for children."

"There are all those things," I said.

She put a very small hand in mine, and I gave her hand a squeeze, and she beamed at me with the largest eyes on earth. "Then I will come with you," she said.

# 12

---

The Russians make dreadful automobiles. The design is inadequate, I suppose, if one prefers to regard an automobile as something that ought to be made purposely lacking in aesthetic appeal. But if the object is to produce purely functional vehicles, then the very least they should do is function. Ours did, but barely. The engine knocked, the crankcase leaked oil, and the few modest hills we climbed were an enormous strain on the poor thing. The only good thing to be said for the car was that some poor fool had left the key in the ignition, and I had thus been able to steal it without any difficulty whatsoever.

I was driving west, toward the setting sun. Milan sat on the passenger side, and the small object of our conversation was nestled between us, her head resting gently against me.

"You realize," Milan was saying, "that this may be the most profoundly stupid act of your life."

"It may be the last, as far as that goes."

"You joke, but it is no joke. Every step we take we seem to accumulate more paraphernalia. Chinese puzzles, Polish microfilm——"

"Yugoslav refugees——"

"A valid point, Evan. I am the first to admit that my book and I come under the heading of excess baggage, and you know my gratitude to you. But this is plainly impossible. The girl is just a child."

"That's the whole idea."

"Evan——"

"Damn it to hell," I said. "They had the kid locked up in a dungeon. Did you see the way she was squinting at the sunlight? Another few years under that kerosene lamp and she'd have been blind as a bat. She's a bright child, she's a beautiful child, she wants the things every child ought to be able to have, and how in the name of God could I have left her in that cellar with those two crazy old crones?"

"I know, I know."

"As it was, I nearly had to brain Hescha to get her to part with the kid."

"I know."

"What would you have done?"

"The same thing you did," Milan said. "Exactly the same, exactly."

"Then, what's the point?"

"I just wanted you to know that you are crazy, Evan. I never denied that I too am crazy. Why did you steal the car?"

"Because I am crazy."

"Seriously."

"Because I felt like stealing the car," I said. "Because I'm sick of walking and sick of buses. Because we couldn't drag Minna down the road or onto a bus anyway."

"Ah. I thought so."

"We'll get rid of the car in Riga if it lasts that far. And then we'll find out that Sofija is married or dead or whatever, and then you and I and Minna will go to Finland and get a plane for the States. That's why I stole the goddamned car."

The car coughed and sputtered, and I cursed it quietly but firmly in Lettish. At my side Minna stirred and blinked. I pampered the accelerator pedal, and the engine purred again. Milan mentioned that there was a dog in the road. I assured him that I was aware of the presence of the dog in the road but thanked him, regardless, for pointing the dog out to me.

Minna said, "Are you speaking Russian?"

"No, Serbo-Croat."

"Where is that spoken? In America?"

"In Yugoslavia."

"I can read Russian because many of my books are in Russian, but Aunt Hescha told me I was to speak only in Lithuanian. What is spoken in America?"

"A dialect of English."

"They do not speak Lithuanian?"

"No."

"Then they will not be able to understand me?"

"You'll learn English," I said. "I'll teach you."

Her face brightened. Milan asked if it was necessary for us to continue speaking such an impossible language. I assured him that it was. Minna wanted to know when we would be in America.

"Not for a long time," I said. "First we must go to Riga, in Latvia. They speak Lettish there. Do you know of Lettish?"

"No."

"It is very much like Lithuanian, but there are differences. Would you like to learn how to speak it?"

"Oh, yes!"

"It will be easy for you. By the time we reach Riga, you will speak it correctly."

"I will speak Lettish?"

*"Runatsi latviski,"* I said. "You will speak Lettish." I took her hand. "You see how the words change? *Zale ir Zalja*—the grass is green. *Te ir tēvs*—here is father. *Tēvs ir virs*—father is a man. *Mate ir plavā*—mother is in the meadow."

*"Mate ir plava zalja,"* said Minna. Which meant that mother was in the green meadow, and which also meant that Minna was getting the hang of it. We went on talking, and before long I did not translate my little sentences into Lithuanian because she was able to understand them well enough in Lettish. Once she saw the way the nouns and verbs changed slightly, she was able to turn many Lithuanian words into Lettish ones by herself.

The fact that she was a child was enormously helpful. Children are delightful little animals, their minds crisply logical and extraordinarily retentive. They extrapolate and interpolate with ease, they concentrate with uncluttered minds, and they have never learned to make the distinction between work and play, approaching either with the same intent devotion and absorption.

Minna, slipping so readily into the genuine complexities of Lettish syntax, put me in mind of an apothegm of Nietzsche's: "The true maturity of man is to recapture the seriousness one had as a child at play." Why they ever lose it in the first place is the mystery.

*"Varetu runat latviski,"* said Minna, as we reached the outskirts of Riga.

"Yes," I assured her, "you are able to speak Lettish. And very well."

• • •

Riga is an important city, capital of the Latvian S.S.R. and containing nearly three-quarters of a million people, the greater proportion of them Letts. We abandoned our car in a quiet street near the harbor, and I left the key in the ignition so that anyone who wanted to could carry it still farther away from us. We walked together, Milan and Minna and I, through the streets of Riga. But for the utter lack of family resemblance we might have been taken for three generations of a family: daughter and father and grandfather, *meita un tevs un vectevs*. We asked directions and found the address I had memorized. We passed the apartment building where Sofija Lazdinja lived and walked a few yards farther to a cafe. We took a table. I ordered bowls of soup for everyone, told Minna to order anything else she wanted. She had never been in a restaurant before and had not realized there were places where anyone might go to order food. She thought it was a delightful idea. I left the two of them there, amused by the thought that they would be quite unable to talk with one another, and went off in search of Sofija.

A directory inside the door of her building informed me that Lazdinja was apartment 4. I climbed a flight of stairs and found a door with a 4 on it at the end of the corridor. I knocked, and the door opened, and I looked at a face I had heretofore seen only in photographs, and I realized instantly why Karlis had fallen so irretrievably in love with her. The form of a goddess, the face of an angel, sparkling eyes, flashing teeth, red lips . . .

I said, "You are Sofija Lazdinja?"

She said, "No."

I don't think I said anything; if I did, I'm sure it didn't make any sense. I was too busy being astonished. But what she said next was, "I am Zenta Lazdinja. Sofija is my sister. My *older* sister."

"One year older!" This from a voice from within.

**119**

"That is quite true," Zenta said mischievously. "Sofija is only a year older than I. You will find this hard to believe when you see her, but it is true. Only a single year older."

Karlis had not said that there were two of them. Perhaps he had not known. It was almost impossible to believe in the existence of one of them, let alone a matched pair.

"But you have the advantage of us," said Zenta. "You know that I am Zenta and that my older sister Sofija is within, but we do not know your name or who you are."

"My name is Evan Tanner. I have come at the request of a good friend of your sister."

"His name?"

"Karlis Mielovicius."

A shriek from within. "Karlis!" Another goddess rushed into view, pushed Zenta aside, gripped me furiously by the arms. She was an inch or so taller, a shade more voluptuous in physique, and, as I had been repeatedly advised, one year older. "Karlis!" she cried again. "You come from Karlis?"

"Yes."

"He is well?"

"Yes."

"He still loves me?"

"More than ever."

"But he has found another?"

"No."

The pressure increased on my arms. "You are very certain of this?"

"Yes."

"Ahhh!" She released my arms, enveloped me in her own, hugged me to her extraordinary bosom, and very nearly crushed the life out of me. I considered reminding her that I was not Karlis myself, that I was merely his emissary, but for the moment I was unable to say anything at all.

She released me eventually and led me inside. We sat down on a long, low couch, with me in the middle and Sofija and Zenta on either side. And I explained, in a great flow of words, that Karlis wanted her to come to America to be his bride, and that, if this was also her wish, I would do whatever was in my power to take her there.

Evidently it was not something she had to think about for any great length of time. She didn't exactly say that she would like to come. What she said was, "How soon can we leave?"

And Zenta said, "I am coming with you, of course."

"It will be some days before we can leave. Perhaps a week, perhaps longer."

"We can wait. And you may stay here with us, it is safe here."

"There are others with me. An old man and a young girl."

"They will stay with us also."

"And you must not speak a word of this to anyone. It is very dangerous."

"I understand."

"And I too."

"Not a word."

"No. The old man and the girl, where are they?"

"A few doors away," I said. "I will fetch them now."

I hurried back to the cafe. Minna and Milan were at a table where I had left them. The soup bowls were gone—they had shared mine between them, Minna told me—and she was finishing a meal of roast pork while Milan dealt with a meat pie.

I had just enough rubles to cover the check. "We can go now," I told Minna in Lettish. "We can go now," I told Milan in Serbo-Croat.

And that, I thought, was going to be a nuisance. Giving

**121**

everyone directions in a different language and having persons in the party who were unable to communicate with one another could only prove to be a mammoth headache. I've always disliked the notion of Esperanto, feeling that a variety of languages makes the world infinitely more interesting, and to me the myth of the Tower of Babel has always had a happy ending. But now I could somewhat appreciate the desirability of a universal language, if only to be dragged out on special occasions. This, certainly, was one such occasion.

But as we left the cafe and proceeded to Sofija's apartment house Milan said that the food tasted good to him.

I nodded. And then did a monumental doubletake because what he had said, word for word, was *"Man garsho bariba."*

I looked at Milan, who was smiling shyly, and at Minna, who was simply beaming. Esperanto would be unnecessary from now on, as would Serbo-Croat. In a few days the little minx would have him speaking Lettish.

# 13

---

We were about as cozy as a group of five can reasonably expect to be in an apartment designed to accommodate two. I explained that I had no need of a bed, that I could more easily sleep during the day, when the others were up and about, and that most of my planning for the exodus would have to be done at night anyway. Sofija and Zenta, who shared a large bed in the one small bedroom, decided that there was certainly room in that big bed for Minna as well. Milan declared that he would sleep most comfortably on the couch. So the sleeping arrangements were not particularly inconvenient. It was when we were all present and all awake that the apartment was overly crowded. We would sit balancing plates of food on our laps, or stumble about bumping into one another, or merely demonstrate through general discomfort and malaise that the apartment did not fulfill our territorial imperative.

I coped with this situation by carefully being absent at times when everyone else was present. The girls were away most of the day, and it was easy enough for me to invent mysterious missions that would take me out of the apartment during the evenings.

It was easy, in fact, to invent almost anything but an escape route out of Latvia. There were too many of us, and we were too heavily loaded down for us to get out as easily as Milan and I had gotten in. If I had come alone, and if Sofija herself had been alone, a routine of border-hopping and disguises might have worked. Now, with our party of two transformed into a party of five, that was out of the question.

And Minna, delight though she was, constituted another problem. She couldn't be expected to walk long distances or endure much in the way of hardship. She was only six years old.

All of which meant that our departure would have to be swift, bold, abrupt.

And therefore dangerous.

We would need a car for a start. That wouldn't be too difficult, I decided; one of the girls could simply borrow one from a friend (girls who look like that invariably have friends who are anxious to lend them cars), and we could abandon the car when the time came. That, after all, is what friends are for.

With a halfway decent car we could drive from Riga to Tallinn in four hours at the outside. The Estonian capital is on the Gulf of Finland just fifty miles south of Helsinki. The Russians patrol those waters carefully, but no marine patrol can be that perfect, and it seemed reasonable to assume that a fast ship in the hands of an alert and cooperative (and greedy) boatman could get us through.

I was unsure how wide-armed a reception we could expect in Helsinki. The Finns have the good sense to remain on good terms with the Russians. Still, a plea for political asylum had to carry some weight. Of course a plea for political asylum generally entails publicity, and Finland is honeycombed with Russian operatives, so Finland might not be the safest place on earth. But if we could reach an American embassy in Finland, then perhaps...

I spent four fairly rotten days and nights playing with this dilemma. I don't think I would have gotten much sleep during those days even if I had been capable of it. What it came down to, finally, was that Finland was better than any other possibility, but that any serious thought about what to do in Finland had to wait until it was established whether or not we could expect to get there.

None of which could be properly assessed in Riga. So one night, after dinner, I shook hands with Milan, embraced the Lazdinja sisters warmly, kissed Minna, and went to Tallinn.

The waterfront bars in Tallinn are much like waterfront bars at any seaport. Talk of women and ships, heavy drinking, conversations in a dozen languages at once, and underneath it all a healthy disrespect for law and order. Every seaman is, at heart, a smuggler and an anarchist. When a man spends as much of his time sailing on open waters with sailors from all over the world, he learns not to care much about the prevailing governments on that one-fourth of the globe that God, for some mysterious reason, saw fit to spoil by covering it with land.

Waterfront bars are good places. Men drink, men get drunk, men fight, men occasionally kill one another, but a waterfront bar remains a generally good place to be.

I was in just about every damned one in Tallinn. I lived in them until I found my man, and then I spent a long time scouting him and another long time conversing with him. It took a couple of days and nights until I was virtually certain he was right. He had a fast ship, he had no love for any government and liked the Soviet government least of all, and, most important of all, he hungered for money.

I had $1,000 U.S. in a money belt around my waist. The farther one gets from America, the more desirable the U.S. dollar becomes. I felt it ought to be enough to carry the deal. A man with a fast ship of his own in a port like Tallinn is almost certain to be a full-time smuggler, working contraband back and forth between Helsinki and Tallinn. A smuggler is accustomed to heavy profits, but a thousand U.S. dollars for one night's work still added up to a substantial sum. So I waited until we were alone in the night, halfway between one saloon and the next on down the line, and then I made my pitch.

"Ander," I said, "you are an intelligent man. You know this port and these waters. I have a question for you."

He waited.

"Let us suppose, Ander, that there was a family of five, a man and two women and a child and a grandfather, and all of them without papers. Let us suppose that they wanted to go from Estonia to Finland, and to leave Estonia without anyone knowing of it, and then to enter Finland without anyone knowing it. Let us suppose——"

"They would have to go by boat," he said.

"That would no doubt be the best way."

"It would be dangerous. Very few men would have the courage to transport them. And very few families would have the resources to afford such a trip."

Ah, good. We were getting closer to brass tacks.

"Do you think a man with the necessary amount of cour-

126

age could be found? And with the skill and daring to make the trip in safety?"

"It is possible."

"And what resources would the family require?"

"A great deal."

He was a Dutchman or a Lascar or a German or a Spaniard, depending upon his audience and his mood. He was somewhere between thirty and fifty. He was not going to name a price, nor was he going to settle for a sum until he knew it was as much as he could possibly get.

So I said, "Ander, this family would give its entire resources. Everything. Its entire resources amount to exactly one thousand dollars, American. In American bills. Twenty fifty-dollar bills."

"That is not enough."

The inevitable response. "Then, there is no point in our discussing this family further," I said, "because this family never tries to make bargains. This family has precisely the sum of money mentioned, no more and no less, and there is no point in our wasting our time."

And I shook hands warmly with him and went back to the bar from whence I had come.

I outwaited him. It took some doing, because he was fairly certain that I needed him more than he needed me and he was dead right. But I had no more chips left, and the sooner he realized as much, the easier things would be all around. I waited an hour, nursing beers and talking with some Norwegians, and then Ander came in, passed me, brushed my arm with his, and nodded shortly at the door.

I met him outside. In an alleyway he said, "The price is acceptable. The trip is dangerous but may be made safely. We can speak plainly, you and I. How soon can you be ready to leave?"

"A few days."

"The crossing must be made on a Sunday night. It is much simpler and safer then. Tonight is Thursday. Can you be ready Sunday night?"

"Yes."

"And the money?"

"You will be paid when you land us on the Finnish coast."

"And if it turns out that you do not have the money?"

"Then you can shoot us and throw us overboard."

"And if I take the money without delivering you to Finland?"

"Then we can shoot you," I said, "and throw you overboard."

"We understand each other, my friend."

"I think we do."

"For men of intelligence nothing is impossible."

"Nothing."

"I will explain where you must be and at what time. There must be no delays, you understand that. Of course you understand it, I don't have to waste our time." And he explained, in careful detail, just where his boat would be moored in the gulf to the east of the harbor proper. It would be essential that we be there a half hour before midnight Sunday night. No sooner and definitely no later.

We shook hands on the price, the time, the place, and the brotherhood of intelligent men. We had a final drink together. I left him then and spent a few hours trying to decide whether he would feel it was more to his advantage to ferry us across the gulf or sell us down the river. I decided that he would be all right. Not for moral reasons, certainly, but because we had to be more profitable to him on my terms than in any other way. And I was fairly sure he would realize as much; the one thing I trusted about him was his judgment.

· · ·

I took my time getting back to Riga. I wanted a look at the embarkation point before dragging everyone north and I wanted sight of it in the daylight. It wasn't a bad spot, a few miles down the gulf coast. There was a massive industrial complex a few hundred yards away, with a high wire fence around it, but of course it would be sound asleep by Sunday night and no bar to our plans.

I was back in Riga by late afternoon. I'd caught a few decent rides and had been careful not to do too much walking in between. My shoes, I noticed, were getting a little down at the heels, and that was bad; if they wore much more, the cans of microfilm would fall out.

I knew something was wrong the minute I walked in the door. I looked at Zenta and at Sofija and knew something was very wrong, but their faces wouldn't tell me what it was. I looked at Minna, and she made her eyes very wide and nodded toward the sisters. *These people are foolish,* her eyes told me.

"Where's Milan?" I asked.

"He went outside. He was nervous, he went next door for a cup of tea."

This was odd. Milan, however nervous, had the good sense to stay put.

"Evan." Zenta took a step toward me. "I fear I have been stupid. I have done something wrong."

I glanced at Minna, who raised her eyebrows and nodded.

"The other members of our gymnastic troupe," Sofija said. "This one told them of our plans."

"Oh, no."

"Oh, yes. This one, who is a year younger and an eternity stupider, this one with the large mouth——"

"They are sisters to me," Zenta said. "Years we have performed together, always without secrets, always as sisters——"

"There is a time for secrets," I said.

"I know, Evan."

"This was the time, too. How many are there in your troupe?"

"Twelve all told. Sofija and myself and ten others. Twelve good, decent Lettish girls."

"Then, we might as well hang ourselves," I said, "because if ten of them know, five of them will talk."

"Oh, no, Evan."

"It stands to reason, does it not? Of two good decent Lettish girls, one talked. So of the ten remaining..."

I looked at Minna. She was closing her eyes in a burlesque of pain. *It gets worse,* she seemed to be saying. But how?

"They will not talk, Evan." This from Sofija.

"When did they learn?"

"Just a few hours ago, at our daily training period."

"Then at least one of them must have talked already."

"No. None has talked. And none will." Zenta stepped forward, smiling bravely through incipient tears. "Because they are here now, Evan. They all want to come with us, you see, to come with us to America, all of them, and so Sofija said we had to bring them here right away, you see, so that none of them could have the opportunity to be stupid as I am and to tell anyone, and so they are here now and they will come to America with us, Evan."

"They are here?"

"Yes, Evan."

"Here?" I looked around foolishly. "I don't see them."

"They are in the bedroom."

"Ten of them? Ten good, decent Lettish girls in the bedroom?"

"Yes, Evan."

I walked slowly, hesitantly, reluctantly, to the bedroom

door. I took hold of the knob and turned the knob and opened the door.

And they were there, all right.

# 14

---

Milan was in the cafe, lurking morosely over a cup of tea. I hissed to him from the doorway. He looked up, saw me, nodded, put money on the table, and got to his feet. We walked a few yards down the street and turned together into an alleyway.

"You have been upstairs, Evan? You know about them?"

"Yes."

"I will get Minna, we can't leave her behind, and tonight the three of us will leave Riga."

"Impossible."

"First, to prevent disclosure of the fact, I shall personally strangle those twelve idiot girls."

"You are a man of peace, Milan."

"I have never been so provoked. Evan, this is an utterly impossible situation."

"I know."

"You made arrangements in Tallinn?"

I nodded. "For a party of five," I said. "We now seem to be fifteen."

"I propose we once again become a party of three. What sort of arrangements did you make?"

I gave him a quick account of the bargain I had struck with Anders. Milan was surprised to learn that I had a thousand dollars in my possession and a little nervous at the thought of buying our way across. I told him I thought Anders was reasonably safe.

"But fifteen instead of five. Will he take such a party?"

"If not, we can leave the extra girls behind at the last moment. But we have to keep them with us until we go so that no one talks. If he has room for the extras, they can provide some extra money. If not, they can come back to Riga."

"How will we get them there?"

"They said they can get access to cars. Men will lend them cars. We could make the trip in three cars, five to a car."

"I don't like it. I could drive, and you could drive. Can the girls drive?"

"They say they can."

"I still do not like it."

"Neither do I, Milan."

"We will have to think about it." He was silent for a moment. Then he said, "There is only one difficulty with this Lettish language. I do not know the word for manure, and it is not the sort of word I can ask Minna to teach me."

*"Prens,"* I said.

"And horse?"

*"Zirgs."*

*"Zirgs-prens,"* said Milan. "Forty-eight hours before we may leave, in a camped apartment with a dozen women. *Zirgs-prens!"*

• • •

The next day I asked one of the girls—her name may have been Lenja; there were two Lenjas, a Marija, a Natalja, two Katerinas, and a variety of others—about the prospect of acquiring cars. She assured me that it would be no problem at all to get hold of three of them.

I still didn't like the idea of splitting up the group that way. I had considered bundling the ten girls into two cars and sending them scampering off in the wrong direction, a notion that had Milan dancing with glee when I mentioned it to him. The more I thought of it, though, the less I liked it. They were almost certain to get into trouble, at which point they would talk, at which point Russian agents in Finland would know we were coming.

Besides, I couldn't avoid feeling a vague and pointless responsibility for the lot of them. They were, as Zenta had assured me, good, decent Lettish girls. And they did want desperately to get out of Latvia and into America. We were so overburdened anyway that another ten girls couldn't make things too much more difficult. Even if it did, there was something in the idea of liberating an entire gymnastic troupe that appealed to my sense of comedy.

"It could have been worse," I assured Milan. "Suppose Sofija had belonged to the Bolshoi Ballet."

He hadn't thought it was funny.

Now I asked Lenja, or whoever she was, just how the troupe traveled from one engagement to another. There was a private bus reserved especially for their use, she assured me. A driver was provided whenever they had occasion to travel anywhere.

That made it simple. Sunday afternoon Milan and I left the girls with strict instructions to go nowhere and say nothing. Then we went to the garage, knocked the attendant over the head, tied him up, gagged him, locked him in an office, and stole the bus.

We loaded Minna and the Lettish girls into the bus an hour after sunset. I had managed to find a driver's cap and jacket that fit me and I sat in front over the huge steering wheel and piloted the bus through narrow streets to the road to Tallinn. Milan sat directly behind me with Minna at his side. The back of the bus was filled with singing girls, the majority of whom knew only half the words to each song and sang them off-key. A merry group were we.

The bus was an old crate, and I was no bus driver. At first I found myself taking curves at the speed I'd have taken them in an ordinary automobile. This was a mistake—each time it happened, the singing in the rear of the bus was interrupted as the girls were tumbled unceremoniously from their seats. After a few miles I adjusted my driving to the vehicle, and we took it slow and steady into Tallinn. It was almost eleven o'clock when we entered the city. By ten minutes after eleven the bus was parked in a quiet lane just half a mile from the rendezvous point.

"Keep everyone here," I told Milan. "I'll check with Anders and make sure nothing has gone sour. And I'll find out if he has room for fifteen."

"And if not?"

"I think he will. But stay here and keep the girls quiet."

"Of course."

I touched Minna's cheek. "You stay with Milan," I told her. "I'll be back for you as soon as I can. Be a good girl."

"Yes," she said.

I left the bus and walked quickly toward the rendezvous site. I approached from the east, skirting the side of the huge fenced industrial complex, dark and deserted now. I stayed close to the fence and moved quietly down toward the waters of the gulf.

It was hard to see in the darkness. But when I was close

enough, I saw a sleek ship anchored at the water's edge and I sighed heavily and relaxed.

And I crept a little closer and saw another larger ship alongside the first vessel, and a group of men in uniforms, and heard Anders' voice, whining, and heard the crisp orders of the harbor police.

He had not betrayed us. But he had been betrayed himself, or else the harbor police had been after him for some time. It scarcely mattered. As I crouched there watching, Anders was marched off under guard and taken abroad the police vessel. The ship pulled away from the shore, and Anders' own ship, manned by police, followed immediately after it. The two of them disappeared in the blackness of the night, bound for Tallinn Harbor.

Well, that tore it. For a long moment I did not move, did not even breathe. I had fourteen unsafe people sitting in a stolen bus with no place to go. We couldn't return to Riga, we couldn't possibly get through any borders in the bus—we were in trouble. The boat that should have carried us to Finland was gone. The sailor who should have captained that freedom ship was on his way to prison.

And we were going to hell in a haywagon.

We could just drive around in the bus, I thought. One bus, after all, looked rather like another. Or we could send the ten girls back to Riga—they *might* be safe there—and the rest of us could try to get out of the country in a stolen car. I didn't see how it could work, but I didn't see how anything else could work, either, and the longer I stayed where I was, the worse things were going to get. Sooner or later some bright-eyed cop would wonder why a bus was parked on a side street. I had to get back to the bus. I had to do something, anything.

So I retraced my steps, but not slowly now, not slowly at all, but hurriedly, scampering alongside the high wire fence, stumbling, regaining my balance, rushing onward, stumbling once more, brushing this time against the fence . . .

At which point all the sirens in the world began to wail hysterically.

Then everything happened. Searchlights mounted within the industrial complex suddenly sprang to life and focused upon me. Gates swung open, and a handful of armed men streamed forth from within, fanned out in a semicircle, then drew the semicircle close around me. Guns pointed at me. Flashlights flared in my face.

The leader of the group, a heavy, thick-necked Estonian with a machine pistol in his hand, approached me with fury in his eyes. I stood with my hands held high and my brain turned momentarily off.

"You," he shouted. "What are you doing here? What is the meaning of this? Do you not know where you are?"

And, from some far-off corner of my mind, the words of the Chief rushed in to haunt me. *You wouldn't miss a chance at the Colombian job unless it were something very big indeed. There's a missile center outside of Tallinn. Is that part of it?*

"Fool, I'm talking to you! Do you not know where you are?"

I had a fairly good idea.

The bells had stopped ringing, the sirens had ceased to wail, the searchlights were dim once again. And I was inside the gates of the missile complex, inside a large, high-ceilinged building of concrete block. Oil drums and complicated machinery lined the sides of the building, tables and desks were arranged in neat rows at the far end. Overhead, a maze of cables and beams crisscrossed the ceiling.

The same group of men stood around me in the same sort of semicircle. They had holstered their guns now. A quick pat-down had revealed to them that I was not armed, and so they were free to relax.

I, however, was not.

"You say that you are from Latvia."

"Yes."

"But you have no papers."

"No."

"No means of identification."

"No."

"And what were you doing here? Spying?"

"No. Just walking. I did not know of this center, I thought it was merely a closed factory——"

"You were walking in the middle of the night?"

"I wanted to walk down by the water."

"In the middle of the night?"

"I was restless, I could not sleep."

"You were perhaps spying?"

"No, never that."

"Or planning sabotage?"

"Certainly not!"

"Or planning, perhaps, an illegal trip to Finland? Or to receive a shipment of illegal goods from Finland?"

"No."

"It does not matter what you say to me," my interrogator said. "My job is security here, that is all. If what you say is true, you have nothing to fear."

I gave what was supposed to look like a nod of numb relief. The relief was false, the numbness true enough.

"The MVD has been informed. A detachment of their men will arrive shortly to take you away so that your story can be checked. If they release you for a fool or shoot you for a traitor, it is none of my affair. I have merely to guard you until they arrive."

When the MVD checked me, they would find a smuggled

manuscript taped to my body and two rolls of subversive microfilm in my shoes. I did not care to think about what they might do to me. It was like contemplating the various possible manners in which I might eventually die. Such thoughts were not only futile, they were the breeding ground of despair.

I thought instead of fourteen passengers sitting in a darkened bus.

The twelve Lettish girls would have a hard time of it, probably drawing some prison time, possibly getting away with fines and such punishment. Milan Butec would be almost certainly returned to Yugoslavia, where, like Djilas, he would live out his days in prison.

And Minna?

No punishment for Minna, certainly. Adoption, perhaps, by some good patriotic citizens of Soviet Russia. Adoption and relocation in another republic of the U.S.S.R. No trip to America, no chance for her brain to grow the way it wanted to, no opportunity for Minna to become the person she had every right to be.

I could resign myself to the fate of Milan and Sofija and Zenta and the other Lettish gymnasts. I could avoid thinking, at least for the moment, of what might lay in store for me. But I couldn't put Minna out of my mind.

Until I heard a thin, birdlike voice from the far end of the huge room. "Papa? Papa?"

My guards turned toward the voice. And, stepping between two rows of stainless steel desks, her tiny hands clutching a rag doll tight to her chest, her little pink cheeks streaked with tears, came my little Minna.

# 15

---

"Papa!"

"It's his daughter——"

"How did she get in?"

"Papa!"

"Who knows?"

"What a pretty thing she is! The poor child has been crying. Let her go to her father."

"Papa..."

She ran full-speed at me, the little legs flying over the concrete floor. I stooped down and held out my arms, and she threw herself into them. I picked her up and held her close, and she sobbed madly.

"It's all right, Minna," I told her. "Don't cry, it's all right..."

Between sobs she drew something from behind the rag

doll and pressed it into my stomach. My hand closed around it. It was an automatic pistol.

"Hold me in your arms," she whispered urgently. "When you hear a gunshot, get us out of the way as quickly as possible. And shoot as many guards as you can."

"Where did you get this?"

"Milan strangled a sentry."

The guards were chattering as they watched this touching familial scene. "A beautiful child," one said. "How she loves her father."

"He can remember her love in his prison cell."

"What is a child of that age doing awake at this hour? That is what I would like to know."

"Perhaps the whole family was escaping."

"The MVD will be here soon enough."

"Be ready," said Minna.

And a shot rang out at the rear of the hall.

The guards, all but one, spun around toward the source of the noise. The one who did not turn reached for his pistol. I shot him in the chest, grabbed Minna tight, and made a mad dash for a clump of heavy machinery on my right. Bullets splattered the floor around us. We dropped breathless behind a cover of futuristic stainless steel machinery. Minna huddled beside me, and I peered through the machine, took aim, and fired at the man who had asked me all those damnable questions. The bullet went wide. I shot again, aiming for his head, and hit him in the calf. It wasn't the world's best marksmanship, but at least it put the son of a bitch on the ground.

Milan was firing from behind a desk at the far end of the room. He had already done for two of the guards, but there were still almost a dozen of them left, and the odds seemed impossible. There were only two rounds left in my own pistol. I didn't know whether to waste them now or wait until we were rushed.

It seemed hopeless. We were outnumbered and outarmed and outclassed, and our adversaries had help coming; the MVD were due to arrive at any moment. All the guards had to do was keep us pinned down until the secret police arrived in force. Then we would be finished.

I turned to Minna. "How did Milan know I was here?"

"He followed you."

"Followed me?"

"When you left the bus. He told all of us to stay where we were because he had to follow you. He was afraid that there might be a trap, and then he came back short of breath and told us that there had been a trap."

No trap, I thought. Just a maddening combination of little things going wrong, a bit of bad luck for Anders and a bigger bit of bad luck for me.

"He was certain you would be angry with him for disobeying orders," Minna said.

"He picked the right orders to disobey. But I'm afraid it will only make things worse. I don't see how we can get out of here alive."

"Look, Evan—" She pointed at the ceiling. I looked up, and at the other end of the hall Milan shouted, and high up on the ceiling, in the maze of ropes and chains and pulleys and lateral beams, the women's gymnastic team of the Latvian Soviet Socialist Republic swung gaily into action.

They scampered over the ceiling like agile monkeys on the bars of their cages, tossing themselves here and there, then swooping gracefully down upon the guards and soldiers below. They dipped and soared, they swooped and sailed, and the guards didn't know what to make of it.

"Look, Evan!"

Sofija, swinging on a length of wire cable, sailed in a perfect parabolic arc toward a fat bug-eyed guard. He was trying to draw a bead on her with his pistol but couldn't get the gun aimed in time. With one nimble foot she kicked the gun out of his hand. Her other foot took the guard full on the point of the chin and tumbled him out of the game. Another guard crawled on his hands and knees toward the fallen gun. Zenta dropped twenty feet through the air, feet first, and landed with a foot upon each of the guard's shoulders. He crumbled to the floor, and the room rang with the sound of his shoulder bones snapping from the impact.

Minna was dancing beside me, clapping her hands madly in hysterical glee. The guards, the few who were still conscious, had abandoned their guns entirely by now. They were merely trying to get out of the way of the wild Lettish gymnasts.

They didn't have a chance.

Outside, the night once again began to erupt with bells and sirens. Inside the battle was quickly drawing to a close. The plant guards, though not outnumbered, were clearly outclassed; this wasn't the type of situation they had been trained to handle, and the girls were too much for them. Within minutes it was over, and Minna and I emerged from our hiding place and stepped over the inert bodies of the guards. The final score stood at Christians 14, Lions 0. One of our girls—Lenja, I think—had turned an ankle in the course of the fray. She limped slightly. And that, incredibly, was the extent of our injuries.

The girls were beaming with pride. Milan, an odd smile on his round face, moved toward me. "I violated orders," he said apologetically, "because I suspected a trap."

"No trap. The harbor police picked up Anders, and then I blundered into this mess."

"And now?"

**144**

"We have to get the hell out of here. The MVD is on the way. God alone knows what's going on outside."

"Shall we run for the bus, Evan?"

"And then what? The bus won't get us out of Russia."

"We could hide."

"Where?"

"I don't know."

I tried to think straight and couldn't get anywhere. We were in the building, and the building was locked, but sooner or later someone would come and find a way to get in. If we opened the door now, they would all stream in and . . .

And we would all stream out.

That seemed fair enough for openers. I went to the door, opened it. A small gang of troops stood at the ready in front of the door. Other than that, the place was surprisingly quiet. Only the wail of a siren in the distance broke the quiet of the night.

The MVD, I thought. On their merry way.

I glowered at the batch of troops. "About time you got here," I snapped.

"But we have been here all along. The door——"

"Hurry," I said. "Inside, quickly!"

They rushed inside. I scooped up Minna, and as the men rushed inside the rest of us hurried outside and closed the door.

Now what?

On the outside wall of the building there was a glass-enclosed box with a little hammer beside it dangling from a chain. A fire alarm, I thought brightly. I wondered what the penalty might be for turning in a false alarm in Estonia. It did not seem likely to be the greatest of our worries and, if nothing else, it ought to engender a certain amount of immediate confusion. If there was one thing we needed, it was confusion. It could only help us.

I didn't bother with the little hammer. Instead I smashed the glass front with the butt of my pistol and reached through the broken glass to yank the little red lever.

At which point all hell broke loose. Every light in the base went on, and men poured out of every building. They did not come for us, nor did they run to the source of the alarm. In fact they ignored us entirely. They ran in all different directions, some of them dressing as they ran. Mechanics wheeled out fuel tanks, crews righted missiles on their launching pads, and everyone bustled about doing various important tasks.

Milan asked me what the hell was going on.

"I'm not sure," I said. "But——"

"Yes?"

"It looks to me as though they're...well...taking up battle stations. Finding their posts and waiting for further orders from up above."

"I don't understand."

"I don't think that was a fire alarm box."

"Then——"

"I think I've just put the whole base on Red Alert," I said. "I don't know if that was a good idea or not."

The Russians probably call it something other than Red Alert. But whatever they called it, the entire place was quite definitely on it. Planes sat with their engines on, missiles were poised on launching pads, and all around us all manner of furious activity went on.

We, on the other hand, did nothing. We stood around stupidly, all fifteen of us, while the rest of the base very busily ignored us. It was a pleasant state of affairs, but one that seemed unlikely to last for very long. Every base has a commander, and every commander, however incompetent, must sooner or later become aware of two men, twelve women, and a child standing like sheep in the midst of meticulous preparations for World War III.

I wondered suddenly whether I had managed the neat trick of starting a war. I had started a local revolution once, in Macedonia, but that was not at all the same thing as sending Soviet missiles streaming toward Washington and New York. Of course it couldn't happen; the Russians would have built-in safeguards to prevent such a thing. One couldn't honestly launch a global conflict by turning in a false fire alarm.

Still . . .

"What shall we do now, Evan?"

I turned to Milan. "I don't know," I said.

"We ought to do something."

"Yes."

"The bus?"

I gave him a suggestion concerning the bus that carried overtones of a warmer relationship between himself and the bus than in fact existed. He manfully ignored my suggestion and waited for me to think of something a bit more practical.

"Forget the bus," I said this time. "We need something fast, something dramatic, something to slash through all this miasma and get us straight to where we're going. A straight line. Shortest distance between two points. Except the shortest distance isn't always a straight line, sometimes it's a circle. Great circle routes and all that. Flat Earth Society doesn't believe in them, of course, but fly right over the poles. One, two, three and hello, Alaska. Oh, for God's sake!"

"Evan?"

"Follow me," I called out. And without knowing quite where I was going, I began dashing at top speed across the asphalt surface of the missile base.

They followed me.

So did a great many pairs of alien eyes. We could not have looked as though we belonged in those surroundings and we did not draw stares. Everyone seemed to have something else to do, though, and no one made any attempt to find out who we were or where we thought we were going. There were no idle hands about, and the Devil's work remained undone.

We ran. We dodged fuel trucks, circled around little gangs of mechanics and ground crew men. We ran, and I led, and everyone followed, and I wished to hell I knew just what it was I was looking for. A plane, of course. A plane that could take us out of Russia and back to America. A good, fast plane that would get us up and out before anyone could figure out what we were doing. But all the planes were manned with huge crews, and I couldn't imagine how we could capture one or do anything with it once we did. It had been miracle enough that I had driven our bus from Riga to Tallinn; piloting a jet from Tallinn to Alaska was too much to expect.

And then, at the far end of the field, I saw something unlikely. A huge plane, its engines running, its wings swept back at acute angles, its body positioned almost vertically for takeoff.

This in itself was not so odd. But this plane, instead of being surrounded by a humming crew of fliers and mechanics, was almost untended. One man, wearing boots and a heavy flying suit and holding a helmet by its strap, stood at its side smoking a cigarette. He was the only person within fifty yards of the aircraft.

Why?

I ran to him, and the rest of the company followed in turn. I had my pistol in my hand but wasn't quite sure what on earth I could do with it. Shoot the man, I suppose, and then try to fly the plane. But that seemed somehow mindless.

He looked up at our approach, took a last bored drag on his cigarette, and flipped it away. I couldn't think of an even vaguely intelligent opening line.

"You," I snapped in Russian, "what are you doing?"

It should have been his question to me, since I was the one who was behaving oddly. But he did not appear to think of this.

"I'm following stupid orders," he said.

He was very young, early twenties, with a mop of disarranged black hair, deep, dark eyes, and the pointed face and long nose of a Liverpool singer.

"Stupid orders," he said again. "Why do they always have to hold these stupid drills in the middle of the night? If the Americans attack us, it will not be in the middle of the night. The Americans are not crazy. They will come at a sensible hour. So why have drills at this hour?"

Then I hadn't started a war; they were used to drills of this nature. That was comforting.

"And why, if they must have these drills, must I be a part of them? My plane is experimental. There are no bombs on it, only space for bombs. I have no navigator, no copilot, no bombardier, no ground crew. Nothing. So should I not be back in my warm bed?"

"Of course."

"But no. Stupid orders! I must come here, I must start my engines, I must be in my flying suit, I must be ready to take off at once. Even if there is a war, I would not take off. I would have nothing to do. Stupid."

"This is an experimental plane?"

He nodded at it. "A bomber. Long range." He launched into a string of statistics that left me with the general impression that the plane would travel very far and very fast, which was just the fate I had in mind for it.

"And you can fly it? You, by yourself?"

"That is my job. I always fly it."

"Without a crew?"

"Crews get in the way."

I raised the pistol. Behind me Milan and Minna and the Lettish girls hovered expectantly. I pointed the pistol at the young pilot, and he seemed to take notice of it for the first time. He did not look frightened, or even intimidated. He looked at the gun, he looked at me.

He looked bored. "Who are you?"

"An American agent," I said. Forcefully, I hope. "I am ordering you to fly us"—I motioned toward the others—"to America. Now."

"You American?" He had switched, incredibly, to English. "You American agent, Joe? No shit?"

I looked quickly around. The world still seemed to be ignoring us. Minna was tugging at my sleeve. Milan was saying comforting things to the Lettish girls. And I was being spoken to in a strange variety of English by a highly unlikely test pilot.

"No shit," he was saying. "You American?"

"Yes."

"I love America," he said. "I, Igor Radek, I love America! Hey, Joe, Charlie Mingus! Thelonious Monk? No shit!"

"No shit."

"Always my dream is to go to America. Play the trombone, right? Hot jazz, real cool music. No shit, some of a bitch!"

"Could you take us there?"

"In this plane?"

"Yes."

"But the authorities——"

"Or would you rather spend the rest of your life following stupid orders?"

"Some of a bitch," he said. "You right, Joe. We go to

America, no sweat, we fly like a bird." He looked past me at the crowd. "All these peoples going?"

"Is there room?"

"No bombs in the plane, no crew in the plane, sure, no sweat, some of a bitch, plenty of room."

"And you could get us to Alaska?"

"No sweat."

"No one could catch us?"

"This plane?" He laughed. "No plane in Russia catch this some of a bitch."

"Then——"

He looked past me. "Hey, Joe, car coming this way. They after you maybe?"

"Maybe."

"Then what we waiting for? Everybody inside. No sweat, some of a bitch, everybody inside!"

He threw the door open and led the way, and we scurried up the little ladder and into the plane. From the field a man in a jeep was shouting at us through a bullhorn. Igor Radek shouted, "Drop to dead, you some of a bitch!" And, the last of us inside the bomber, he shut the hatch.

# 16

---

The plane in which we were all huddled was an experimental fighter-bomber. Military experimentation, we have long been told, leads inevitably to progress in civilian living—peace-time uses of atomic power, as an example. Sooner or later, then, the great advances exemplified by our Russian fighter-bomber would bear fruit in comparable advances in commercial aircraft.

Such an interpretation seemed highly theoretical to me. Our aircraft struck me as several light-years away from adaptation to comfortable commercial flight. The operative word was *comfortable*; the plane simply wasn't.

We were loaded into the bomb compartments. The bombs, had the plane been carrying them, would have been strapped carefully into place. Otherwise, subjected to the stresses and strains that faced the plane's passengers, the bombs would have delivered their payload immediately upon takeoff.

Which is very nearly what happened to us.

At one moment we were perching precariously in the bomb compartments and trying to ignore the fact that the men on the ground were presently surrounding the airplane. And at the next moment, after Igor had increased engine speed and made a bevy of adjustments to the plane's forbidding instrument panel, and after he had flipped one final lever, we were hurled abruptly into space. No gentle taxiing down the runway, no meticulous countdown to zero in a heavy German accent, no television cameras to increase the moment of drama. No warning at all, really. Just sudden, wild, wholly unanticipated movement.

The girls began to shriek. Milan, evidently convinced that what goes up must come down and that what goes up violently must come down violently, had wrapped his head inside his coat in the manner of a turtle withdrawing into its shell. And Minna, small and soft in my arms, looked up at me and asked me calmly how long it would be before we reached America. She knew nothing about planes, and thus it had not occurred to her that they were something to be afraid of.

"I don't know," I told her. "Not too long."

"And where will we go when we arrive, Evan?"

"To jail."

"Jail?"

"A joke. I don't know, Minna. We shall see what happens when the time comes."

"Why are the Lettish girls screaming, Evan?"

"Perhaps they are excited to be going to America."

"But why should they scream?"

"They don't seem to be screaming much any more."

"No," she agreed, "they have stopped."

They had stopped because the acceleration wasn't so pronounced anymore; we had broken the sound barrier and

**154**

were evidently rather close to our cruising speed. I didn't want to think about our probable cruising speed. I know how fast planes can go and how high they can fly and I find all of this very interesting, but when I am in one of them I prefer to think of other things until I am on the ground again.

"Evan? When you were talking with the man, I could not understand. Was that Russian?"

"At first we spoke Russian, but then we switched to English."

"That was English?"

"A form of English, Minna."

"Oh," she said. "And I will learn to speak it?"

"Yes."

"Some of a bitch?"

I closed my eyes for a moment. When they were open again, I said, "Perhaps you should not pay too much attention to the way Igor speaks English. He is not that good at it." I thought for a moment. "Some of a bitch—actually it should be *son* of a bitch—well, it isn't a very good thing to say. Several of Igor's expressions are not especially polite."

"Like *zirgs-prens?*"

"Did Milan——"

"I asked him what it meant, and he said it was not a polite word to say, but he says it all the time. There are some things I do not understand, Evan."

*Zirgs-prens*, I thought. Some of a bitch. I said, "I think I ought to go up and have a talk with Igor. Find out how we're doing. You wait right here, all right?"

"Yes, Evan."

I stopped first to check on the girls. Some of them seemed a little shaky still from the takeoff, which they had plainly not expected, but Zenta assured me that they were all quite all right. No bruises, no broken bones, just an occasional case of rattled nerves.

Sofija, meanwhile, was telling them about Karlis and his friends in the Latvian Army-In-Exile. "Tall men and strong," she said, "and all of them hard workers, and with good jobs, and pension plans and insurance and Social Security and Medicare. And many of them without wives, and anxious to marry Lettish women, but where are they to find Lettish women in America? But when we arrive..."

Even the most anxious of them calmed down at the thought. Ears perked up, and eyes brightened. A woman will adjust to any peril at the thought of a husband at the end of the rainbow.

And not merely a husband—

"Washing machines," Sofija was saying. "Automobiles, new large ones, a car for the husband and another car for the wife. Television sets, color television sets, and all sorts of different channels to watch. If you do not like one program, you switch the channel, and there is another!"

The American dream, I thought.

"And fur coats! And dresses from Paris and houses with more bedrooms than people and a bathroom for every bedroom and wall-to-wall carpeting..."

I checked Milan, who was still huddled inside his coat. I asked him if he was all right. He mumbled something unintelligible. I checked to make sure there was nothing wrong with him. He seemed healthy enough, just violently upset by the entire concept of air travel. I left him then and moved up out of hearing range of Sofija's reverie of life in America. I hoped the girls would not be unduly disappointed when they were married to the men of their dreams and ensconced in little semidetached row houses in Flushing.

There was a co-pilot's seat vacant next to Igor. I eased

**156**

myself into it and strapped myself in place. He turned to me, eyes radiant.

"See, Joe? What I tell you? No sweat."

"Do we have enough fuel?"

"Plenty fuel, Joe. Enough fuel to go to Washington and back, exactly."

"Washington and back," I echoed.

"Takes less fuel to come back than to go there, Joe."

"Why?"

"Lighter coming back. No bombs."

"Oh."

"You say Alaska?"

"That's right."

"No shit, Joe. I mean, no sweat. We go right up north to the North Pole and then we keep going. I find us Alaska, Joe. Not to worry, no sweat."

"By now they probably have pursuit planes after us," I said.

"Not to worry, Joe."

"But they must know we're leaving, they won't just let us zip up and leave."

"Nobody can catch this some of a bitch, Joe." He patted the dashboard lovingly. "No plane like it. Fastest fighter-bomber in the some of a bitch Air Force."

One of the instruments was making a blipping noise. Radar, I thought, was supposed to make blipping noises. Probably just telling Igor that the ground was still where it was supposed to be. I remembered my first jet flight, when I saw flames leaping from one of the engines and was certain that this ought to be brought to the attention of the pilot. I did not bring it to his attention, and learned subsequently that that sort of thing always happened. Not to worry, no sweat.

"Everybody all right back there, Joe? All hunky-dory?"

"Everyone's fine," I said.

"Those girls aren't Russian, are they? Don't talk Russian, Joe. Or English either."

"They are Lettish," I said.

"Some bunch of broads," he said. "No shit, Joe. Some tomatoes."

Lettish tomatoes, I thought hysterically. A Baltic salad. What other ingredients could we have? Cole slaw? We had a fairly Cold Slav in Milan. Chickory? Chickory chick, cha-la, cha-la . . .

I told myself sternly to stop it. And I listened to the blipping noise on the dashboard. The blips appeared to be coming closer together now.

"You're positive no one could catch us," I said.

"No sweat, Joe." He laughed. "You know what this plane is? This is the MIXK-One fighter-bomber. Only one of its kind in Russia."

"And there's no faster plane?"

"Just the MIXK-Two fighter. Same type of engine, Joe, but smaller. Just one of them in Russia."

"Just one of them?"

"Just one some of a bitch. Alexei Bordunin flies it. Showoff some of a bitch. Yes sir, no sir, showoff Smart Alex."

"And it's faster than this plane?"

"Just a tiny faster, not to worry."

"Well," I said, "I think it's chasing us now. Those blips"— I pointed to the radar screen, or whatever it was—"could that be, uh, Alexei?"

Igor's eyes narrowed. He pursed his lips, studied the instrument panel, paid special attention to the blips. "Some of a bitch," he said softly.

"It's him?"

"Nobody else that fast. Show off cogstocker."

"Will he catch us?"

"Try to capture us," he said. "Still over Soviet territory. Try to force us down, make us do a landing."

"But we can't——"

"Showoff some of a bitch. See this? I flip this switch, Joe, it flaps the ailerons. Let him know we surrender."

"But——"

"No sweat, Joe. You tell everybody to sit tight. Tell the broads Igor says be cool. We go to turn around the plane."

In Lettish I told everyone to hold on tight while we circled. Mercifully, no one asked why. Igor did something with a stick, and the plane swung round in a lazy half-circle.

"There he come! You see him, Joe?"

Through the cockpit shield I could see something small coming toward us, getting rapidly larger. We seemed to hover in the air while the object approached. It was difficult, at that range, to be certain that it was a plane, but as it came closer it was recognizable as such.

"Some of a bitch," Igor was mumbling intensely. "Ho, boy, Alexei cogstocker. Boast about the fast plane, boast about all the girls, Alexei cogstocker. See who laughs the last time, you some of a bitch. Watch, Joe!"

He pressed a pedal on the floor of the plane. There was a brief rumble beneath us, and then, the pursuing fighter abruptly disintegrated.

"Take to that, Alexei cogstocker, some of a bitch! Take to that, boasting crud! Take to that!"

He laughed and laughed and laughed. Then, with a half-sigh, he swung the plane around again and headed once more for the North Pole.

"Lucky I guessed right," he said after a while, when there were no more annoying blips on the radar screen.

"What do you mean?"

"The pedals. Couldn't remember which one delivered the rockets. The plane is always loaded with some of a bitch rockets, but I never use them in experimental flying. Two pedals, one is rockets, one is not. I pick the one on the left, and goodbye Alexei!"

"What does the other pedal do?"

"Delivers the bombs. But we got no bombs, Joe, so——"

"The girls," I said quietly.

"No sweat, Joe. I pick the right pedal."

"The girls," I said, "would have been scattered all over Russia."

"I pick the right pedal, Joe."

I closed my eyes for a few seconds. I opened them. Then, without saying any more, I opened my seat belt and went to the back of the plane to see how everyone was getting along. They were all still there. Igor had picked the right button. Or pedal, or whatever.

Minna wanted to know what had happened. I gave her a much-abridged version, careful not to mention how close she had come to leaving the plane ahead of schedule. I told her simply that another plane had tried to catch us, a bad plane, and that Igor had blown it to bits with a rocket.

She was delighted. She wanted to know how to express enthusiasm in English if one couldn't say *son of bitch*. I told her *hooray* or *jolly good show* or *fabulous* were all acceptable to varying degrees in various parts of the English-speaking world.

"Hooray! Jolly good show! Fabulous!"

The Lettish girls had fallen silent; one or two of them seemed to be sleeping. Milan had withdrawn entirely into his coat and might have been sleeping himself. I bundled Minna up warmly and suggested she take a nap. She smiled up at me and gave me a kiss and closed her eyes.

**160**

Then I went up front again to watch Igor fly the plane.

"Hey, Joe? That's Alaska down there."

"How do you know?"

"Oh, I used to fly over Alaska all the time," he said. "All the time fly over some of a bitch Alaska. Take pictures, you know. Where you want to land? Air base?"

"Could you find one?"

"I know where they are, Joe. No sweat. Big one near Fairbanks. No sweat."

He did something to slow us down, then headed the plane downward. How he found the base, I have no idea. Evidently he had flown over it often enough in the past. Perhaps our radar defenses are not as foolproof as we like to think. They're a good deal better over Air Force bases, however; as soon as the big airfield came into view, so did a great many U.S. planes. Some of them roared up at us and hovered around us.

"I could shoot those some of a bitches down," Igor said.

"Don't."

"I won't."

Other planes roared past us. For a moment I couldn't imagine where they were going. Then I figured it out.

They were going where we had come from.

"Land as quickly as possible," I said. "Someone has to tell those planes to come back."

"No sweat, Joe."

Landing was a much less furious matter than take-off. Igor might have been a nitwit in certain other areas, but he was an expert when it came to flying a plane. He set the fighter-bomber neatly down, taxied the length of the runway, and came to a smooth stop. The plane was instantly surrounded by at least a hundred armed men.

"What next, Joe?"

"Now we get out."

161

"Snow out there. It'll be cold."

"It would be cold anyway," I said. "They might not be too glad to see us."

I was the first one out, with Igor right behind me and the Lettish girls following in turn. Everyone was staring hard at all of us, and especially at the girls. I picked out the clown with the most gold braid on him and went straight for him. I asked him briskly who was in command, and he said he was.

"Then you'd better call those planes back," I said. "This isn't an invasion, it's a rescue mission."

"What the hell," he said. But then he turned to someone and gave an order, and someone ran off to get on the radio.

"And who in hell——"

"This is Colonel Igor Radek of the Soviet Air Force," I said, pointing to Igor. I didn't know whether he was a colonel or what, but it seemed no time for vagueness. "He is claiming political asylum and is delivering to the U.S. Air Force the only existing specimen of the MIXK-One fighter-bomber."

"What in——"

"No shit," Igor said.

"And these are twelve members of the Women's Gymnastic Team of the Latvian Soviet Socialist Republic," I went on. "They are also claiming political asylum. They are also freezing, as are we all. Could we get inside where it's warm?"

"Just a minute. Who the hell are you?"

"An American citizen," I said. "My name is Evan Michael Tanner. That's all I can tell you."

"What?"

I was suddenly very weary. "Let's all go inside," I said again. "Inside, where it's warm. It's not very warm out here, is it?"

"Listen, fellow——"

"You'll want to call wherever it is that you call when something odd happens. Washington, I suppose. Just tell them my name. It may take a while, but sooner or later some idiot will come up here with a gum wrapper, and then everyone will know that everything is all right, and then I can go home."

"I don't get it."

"Nobody does. Let's go inside."

We went inside. It was much warmer there, and that helped. None of us had been dressed for Alaska. Igor was in fairly good shape in his flying clothes, but the rest of us were completely unprepared for the cold.

"Now let's hear it, Tanner."

"You already heard it," I said. "Get on the phone and tell them my name. Tell them I wouldn't tell you any more than that. And if some Ivy Leaguer hands you a gum wrapper, read what's on the back of it. It might be important."

# 17

---

This time there were no cute little Ivy Leaguers with gum wrappers. This time there were some high-level messages sent to and from Washington, and evidently the news got to the chief at the right time, because the Base Commander came up to me before long with a bemused expression on his face.

"Tanner," he said, "I'm not entirely sure who you are——"

Neither was I.

"——but you're pretty well connected, I'll say that for you. The gymnastic troupe gets on a special plane tonight for New York. They'll be met by some attachés from the Athletic Division of the Cultural Exchange Mission of the State Department, whatever the hell that means. They'll be in good hands, I gather. I suppose State will want to run a lot of publicity on this."

"I suppose so," I said.

"That idiot pilot stays here with us while some aviation experts have a look at his plane. He'll go through a full debriefing. We have men who can speak Russian, of course——"

"He speaks English."

The commander looked at me. After a few seconds I looked away. Some of a bitch, I thought.

"He'll undergo a debriefing. So will Butec, in Washington. The State Department section on Yugoslav affairs wants to have a long talk with him. Then there's supposed to be something about a book——"

"He's planning to write a book."

"Whatever the hell it is. But you, you're a special class. They're sending a plane for you, Tanner. It'll be here in a couple of hours. Very hush-hush. I don't even know just who it is you work for, but they'll have a plane here in a few hours and whisk you away to never-never land, for all they care to tell me about it."

"Fine."

He studied me. "You don't *look* important," he said.

I eyed the gold braid, the white hair, the erect military bearing. "You do," I said.

"Eh?" He frowned, puzzled. "You undercover types," he said. "Don't pretend to understand you."

"We're just ordinary fellows."

"Uh." He sighed. "Well, you might as well make yourself comfortable. I usually have a little Scotch about now. Care to join me?"

"I'd like that."

He poured Scotch for each of us. I finished mine first, and he poured me another.

"Tanner? You know, there are two CIA men outside who want to talk with you."

"What did Washington say?"

"That CIA wasn't to be allowed to see you."

"Well," I said, "then that's the answer."

He whistled softly. He was becoming more and more deeply convinced of my importance by the minute. I, on the other hand, did not feel very important at all. I hadn't done anything, really. I just kept being in the wrong place at the wrong time and I kept accumulating more things and people and now I'd brought them all along with me. I could appreciate the fact that all of this would have been quite brilliant had I planned it. But I hadn't and I didn't feel brilliant. Just exhausted. And thirsty—I freshened my drink.

"You must be tired, Tanner. Incidentally, what am I supposed to call you? Just plain Tanner? Nobody said anything about rank, and I don't suppose you people carry military ranks, or maybe you do, I'm not really at all familiar with your type of show..."

His voice trailed off quietly. If I was all that important, he seemed to be saying, there ought to be something more to call me than just my last name.

"Tanner is fine," I assured him. "That way I'll always know who you mean."

"Uh. Well, fine, Tanner, fine. Listen, you must be dead on your feet. That plane won't get here for a few hours yet. Want to grab a little shut-eye?"

"Thanks just the same, but no."

"A few hours sleep never hurt anyone."

"Not just now."

"Keyed up, eh?" He grinned. "You're a cool bunch, you people, but I guess you're as human as the rest of us. I'll get out of your way, Tanner. And"—he abruptly thrust out his hand, and I, after a moment's stupidity, took it and shook it—"just let me say I'm proud to know you, Tanner. You're all right. And what you did was, well—"

I got rid of him as quickly as I could. The plane would

167

arrive in a couple of hours, and I had things to do. I had to tell the girls how much of their story to give out with and I had to explain to Milan that he had not yet written that book of his. If they knew it existed in manuscript form, they would want to have script approval rights. It would be far better to greet them with a *fait accompli*.

I also had to get those Chinese documents from Milan. We went to the lavatory together and we untaped the packets and added them to the load I was carrying. I didn't want those Chinese documents getting into the wrong hands, not until I could find out what the hell they were.

"Tell them as little as possible," I told Milan. "Don't mention the Polish microfilm or Minna or the Chinese garbage or anything. Pretend you don't understand the questions. Just keep insisting that you want to get to New York and work on your book in peace. Tell them——"

"You do not have to explain, Evan." He smiled brightly. "I will tell them just what I would tell any government. I will tell them nothing."

"And call me in New York."

"How will I reach you?"

"I'm in the Manhattan phone book."

"Very good."

Then I collected Minna, and we waited for the plane.

We didn't have to wait very long. After an hour or two someone in a uniform came along and told us that our plane had arrived. Minna was sleeping soundly. I carried her to the plane. There were two men on board, neither of whom I recognized. One of them said, "Tanner?" I nodded, and he told me to climb aboard. I carried Minna inside and put her in a seat and belted her in. I sat down next to her.

"No one said anything about a kid," the man said.

"So?"

"Nothing," he said, and we took off.

I don't know where we flew, how high or how far or how fast or even what direction. The windows of the plane were entirely blacked out except for the cockpit, and the door to the cockpit was closed. After a while Minna woke up and wanted to know where we were. I told her we were on another plane but that we were in America now, still. If we were in America, she said reasonably, then why did I not speak to her in English?

"Because you do not understand English," I said.

"Can you not teach me?"

The plane ride, with no possible view through the blacked-out windows and no notion of where we were going or when we would get there, was exceedingly monotonous. The monotony was considerably lightened by the game of teaching a difficult language to an eager pupil. English syntax varies considerably from Lithuanian and Lettish, but a child's mind is nicely equipped to bridge gaps of that sort.

"Hand," I said, touching her hand.

"Hand," she repeated dutifully.

"Minna's hand."

"Minna's hand."

"Minna's face."

"Minna's face."

"Minna's arm."

"Minna's arm."

"Minna's foot."

"Minna's foot."

"Evan's foot."

And so on. By the time the plane landed, she had a working knowledge of the parts of the body and the articles of clothing, plus an understanding of the way possessives are formed in English, plus a surface acquaintance with the present tense of the verb *to be*. Most important, she spoke a clean English, with no discernible European accent. Because she was a child and a natural mimic, she duplicated my speech exactly rather than coloring her words with a Baltic accent. She had learned Lettish in a few hours; it would not take her more than a few weeks to learn English.

Well. The plane landed, and the door to the cockpit opened, and one of the men motioned for me to follow him. "Minna's foot," said Minna, and placed it upon the floor of the plane.

"Evan's arms," I said, lifting her in them and carrying her off the plane. I set her down upon the ground.

"Minna's foots," she said. Then, correcting herself, "Minna's *feet*," and began walking with them.

"Minna's hand," I said, holding out mine. She took it, and we followed our man down a tree-lined path toward a small concrete block building.

We were somewhere in the country, somewhere in deep woods adjacent to a private flying strip. That was as much as I could tell. Our man rang a bell, and another man opened a door. This man was one I had seen before, in Washington. His name was Joe Klausner, and he had liberated me from a jail cell in the basement of the CIA offices.

"Tanner," he said, and gave me a smile. "Hello," he said, and smiled at Minna. "Go right inside," he said. "The Chief's waiting for you." He took the arm of the man from the plane, and the two of them walked away.

We went inside. There was a fireplace with logs burning furiously within it, and there were four massive leather chairs, and there was a rough oak table with a bottle and two glasses on it.

And in one of the chairs, filling the glasses from the bottle, was the Chief.

I had never seen any man look happier.

"A favor for a friend," he said. "Just an errand for a

friend. I knew you were onto something big, Evan, but Lord knows I never dreamed it was this big." He began to chuckle. "Good they called those SAC planes back in time. I'm afraid you gave some of those military types a scare. Serves them right, I'd say. Can't hurt to test our automatic recall system now and then. But it would have been a bit much"—another involuntary chuckle—"if you'd had us bombing Moscow. Not quite what peaceful coexistence is all about, eh?"

We were on our second round of drinks. During the first I had tucked Minna into one of the leather chairs and suggested in Lettish that she take a little nap. When she said she wasn't sleepy, I advised her to pretend to take a nap, and she thought that was a fine idea. Either she was an excellent actress or the pretending had turned into reality.

The Chief had wanted to know who Minna was, and I explained that she was just a child who had gotten in the way and whom I had taken along for the ride. I would take care of her, I assured him, and he needn't worry about her overhearing anything, as she didn't speak English.

Then he fussed with the fire some, and we talked about trivia and we finished that first pair of drinks and he poured out a second round. Now it was time to Discuss Things.

"A favor for a friend," he said again. "I've learned to expect great things from you, Tanner, but this almost exceeds believability. The entire Latvian Women's Gymnastic Team fleeing Russia to seek political freedom in the West. Most extraordinary propaganda coup in ages. We're happy enough with the occasional ballet dancer or violinist, and they've been rare enough lately. But they can always be explained away as isolated malcontents, neurotics." He sighed heavily. "When you have an even dozen beautiful girls, though, then you have really got something."

There was no argument there.

"One of them was the sweetheart of a friend, is that right?"

"Yes."

"So that gave you an opening, and then you were able to convince the rest to come along. Rather an astonishing bit of persuasion, I'd say."

I remember walking into that flat in Riga and learning that ten extra girls were sardined in the little bedroom, ready to join us. Astonishing was the operative term, all right.

"And Milan Butec," he went on. "Of course he was the prime reason for your trip. That was instantly obvious. When a resistance hero and leading minister of a communist country is anxious to defect, that's the time to pull out all the stops and go in there and get him."

"Of course."

"But your sources of intelligence are extraordinary, Tanner. We thought we knew pretty well what was going on in Yugoslavia. The country's in a constant state of ferment, needless to say, but our own intelligence posts within that country are rather good. At least I thought they were good."

"Sometimes it's hard to know everything that's going on," I said helpfully.

"Not a word about Butec. Not a single word."

"Well——"

"And yet you knew well enough in advance to plan a careful trip in there and get him out. The Foggy Bottom boys will be having the time of their life with him right now, you'd better believe it. Understand he's going to be writing a book?"

"That's right."

"Probably want to publish it under USIA auspices. They'll want to make sure the thing has just the right slant. The ideal tone, that is."

*Zirgs-prens,* I thought. But what I said was, "Butec

seemed a bit worried about that, you know. Wants to make sure the book is just the way he wants it."

"They often take that line."

"Yes. But what I suggested was that I might do the translation, you see. That way it would come out just right, and of course there would be no question of State Department manipulation."

"And he agreed?"

"He's all in favor of it, yes."

He beamed at me. "Couldn't ask for better than that. He'll be happy, the public will be sold, and we'll be sure of getting just the right sort of, uh, translation."

They'd get just the right sort of, uh, translation, all right. They'd get an exact and faithful rendering of Butec's book, word for lovely word. Whether they liked it or not.

"But what I can't understand," he went on, "is how on earth you got that plane out in the bargain. Only one of its kind in the world, you know. I understand Air Force Intelligence has been trying to smuggle a man into the Tallinn base for months just to get a look at the damned thing, maybe a stray bit of blueprint or something. Instead we wind up with the whole plane. And the one man who's been flying it. Understand he's a little bit of a madman. Is that right?"

"He's a bit odd," I admitted.

"Which of course gave you your opening. It must have taken weeks of preparation to con him into defecting. You're quite the expert at getting people to do what you want them to do, aren't you, Tanner?"

"Well, he wants to play trombone in an American jazz band, actually."

"And you hooked onto that and turned him from a malcontent into a defector. Good piece of work."

I paid attention to my drink.

"Something I heard, Tanner. You were pursued by the sister plane of the MIXK-One, is that right? The MIXK-Two, the fighter, that would be."

"Yes."

"Our military intelligence must be wrong, then. According to what we have, the fighter's the faster of the two and a bit more maneuverable."

"It's faster," I said. "Igor, uh, the pilot, shot down the pursuit plane."

"Shot down the MIXK-Two?"

"With rockets. It, uh, disintegrated."

"So we stole one plane from them and blew the other one to hell and gone. And their pilot with it, of course."

Alexei, I thought. That cogstocker.

"Stole one plane and blew up the other one," he said. He got to his feet, glass in hand, and walked over to where a window might have been had the little building been equipped with windows. He tapped his glass idly against the wood paneling that was hiding the fact that we were in a sort of above-the-ground bomb shelter. He sipped his drink, shook his head, and went on speaking to the wood-paneled wall.

"Stole one plane, blew up another plane. Helped a top Yugoslav to defect, got translation rights to his book. Slipped an even dozen Latvian gymnasts into the States." He turned to me. "You wouldn't have any extra surprises for me, would you, Tanner?"

I lowered my eyes. I looked at my shoes, their heels fitted with rolls of microfilm from Kracow. I thought of the various packets taped to my skin, Milan's book, the Chinese documents that Lajos had smuggled to me from Budapest. I looked at one of the other plush leather chairs and smiled at the sleeping form of Minna, direct descendant of Mindaugas, first and last reigning monarch of a free and independent Lithuania.

"Nothing else, I'm afraid," I said.

"Well, I'm glad of that. Any more, and I'd have trouble believing it myself." He laughed. "Another drink?"

"Please."

"Just Butec alone would have been ample justification for your trip," he said, pouring. "The rest are delightful dividends. And they reinforce my conviction that the best thing to do with a good agent is to give him his head and stay out of his way. I was desperate to send you to Colombia, but thank the Lord I had the good sense to leave you alone when you turned the job down. I felt you must know what you were doing, and you damn well did."

"Oh," I said, remembering. "Colombia."

"Would have liked to see you have a shot at it, Tanner, but I doubt that you could have done much to change the outcome. The Colombian Agrarian Revolutionary Movement evidently had a much broader base of support than anyone suspected. You might have given them a run for their money, but I think they'd have come out on top at the end."

"They won, then?"

"Oh, yes," he said. "Yes, they did." He dropped into his chair again and put his feet up onto the table. "When you opted out, I didn't have anyone else I wanted to send. Passed the ball back to the quarterback, and it wound up going to the CIA. I was fairly certain the Agency would wind up with it and I wasn't very happy at the thought. They can make a mess of things, you know."

"I know."

"You wouldn't believe what a job they did of this, though. Seems CIA security isn't what it's cracked up to be. I always had the feeling that any broadly based organization like that one had to have a few big leaks in it. Well, this time they leaked all over the floor and then stepped in it. The CARM people had advance word that the Agency was taking over. You may not know it, but the CIA hasn't got the best possible public image in South America."

"Is that so?"

"Well, Cuba and all that. Seems they went in there quietly with a batch of top Washington men and some good counterrevolutionary types who haven't had much work since Batista left Cuba. CARM knew they were coming and spread the word all over Colombia. Most astonishing thing. Minute the Agency came in, popular opinion swung completely to the side of the rebels. Not just the peasantry and the workers, either. We expected that much. But the military went over to CARM as well, and that hardly ever happens. When there's a military uprising, it's almost always right wing."

"I know."

"So what they had was hardly what you'd call a revolution at all. A bloodless coup, really. When you've got the army and the peasantry and the workers all on one side, and nothing but foreign business interests and the CIA on the other side, well, the result is a foregone conclusion. Wasn't completely bloodless, of course. The top government officials got it in the neck. They hanged the dictator, uh, the president, right out in front of the palace. All that money in his Swiss bank account, and he never got to spend it. And then they did put a batch of CIA personnel in front of a firing squad. Mostly the Cubans, the ones from the old Batista regime. Most of the Washington types got back home again." He chuckled. "Though I'll bet some of them would just as soon be dead. I don't think they can hold their heads high right now."

"I can imagine. Then Colombia's gone Communist?"

He thought about this. "Well, not exactly," he said. "You

remember when we discussed the situation, and you said they weren't exactly Commie? Looks as though you were right. They might do a Fidel sooner or later, but right now they seem pretty middle-of-the-road, if you follow me. Of course they're nationalizing the big oil and land interests right and left, and some of our petroleum people aren't exactly thrilled, but they haven't gotten on their knees to Moscow or Peking either. Of course it's too early to tell what'll happen later on."

So CARM had won, I thought. In a way that was the best news of all.

He passed me a fat envelope. "For your expenses," he said. "Don't argue, take it. Your plane's refueled by now. You'll be flown to a private airport on Staten Island and from there you can get back to your home base easily enough." He nodded toward Minna. "She'll be going with you?"

"For the time being."

"Mmmm. Pretty little thing. You'll find a good home for her, of course." He got to his feet. "This Colombia thing didn't turn out all that badly, I don't suppose. The only really rocky thing about it is the security leak at the Agency. Gives them one hell of a black eye. A lot of men are burning to get hold of the bastard who tipped it."

"I don't blame them."

"That's one damned good thing about our own operation, Tanner," he told me. "You'll never find a security leak in our bunch."

"Thank God for that," I said.

# 18

----------------------------------------------------------------

After that things got back to normal, or as close to normal as they generally get. Minna and I flew to some airport in Staten Island, still not knowing in what part of the country the meeting with the Chief had taken place. We went to my apartment, bought some fresh clothes for Minna, and I got to work tying up loose ends.

In among the sacks of mail that had come while I was gone was my passport. It had been mailed from London, and so it was in perfect order except for the lack of an English exit visa stamp. This didn't bother me very much. Passports get stamped all over the place, and no one pays too much attention to the chronological order of things. Besides, the passport was a fake anyway; I'd bought it in Greece some months ago to replace one the Czechs had confiscated from me. It had the right number and photograph, so it couldn't have been any better for me if it had been the original.

Along with the passport was an effusive note from Pindaris. He was enjoying himself in London, he had a good job at a restaurant, and he would love me forever for the great sacrifices I had undertaken on his behalf, as would the entire membership of the Pan-Hellenic Friendship Society, united as we were toward the restoration of Greece to its legitimate historic boundaries, and so on *ad nauseam*.

The Lettish girls went to Providence in a body as soon as the State Department decided to leave them alone. A theatrical booking agent had signed them up, and they were scheduled to embark soon on a tour of the United States with a program entitled Gymnastics and Free Enterprise. They were not quite sure what this meant but did know that their salaries were quite generous. I went up to Providence myself to be best man at the wedding of Sofija Lazdinja and Karlis Mielovicius, a three-day bonanza during which time a great deal of alcoholic beverages were consumed, and of which I have only an imperfect recollection at best. Afterward Zenta came back to New York with me and stayed around for a while before the group went off to play its first engagement in Cleveland.

Igor Radek turned up briefly, unrecognizable in tapered slacks, polkadot shirt, short double-breasted blazer, and mirror sunglasses. He had auditioned successfully for the trombonist slot with a small jazz-rock band that had since landed an engagement at a small club in the Village. An original composition of his was being recorded on the band's first LP; the title, he told me, was *Russian To and Fro*.

Milan Butec is living under an assumed name at a large residential hotel on West 23rd Street and taking a Berlitz course in English and doing fairly well at it. The translation went well, and a friend of mine has a publisher interested.

Milan plans to use the advance to buy a small and unproductive farm somewhere in Virginia or North Carolina. He has learned that he will not have to grow anything on the farm, but will be able to live quite comfortably on the book's future royalties plus the soil bank subsidies he will receive for not growing either tobacco or hogs, depending upon the location of the farm. He already understands the entire farm subsidy program far better than I do and feels that it is marvelous. "A Balkan mind is better equipped to appreciate this sort of program," he has told me more than once. "A Balkan mind must have formulated it originally. Masterful."

The Polish microfilm went to its specified destination, Polish exile leaders in New York and Chicago. They were glad to receive it and happy to have word that Tadeusz was alive and well; they had heard he had been executed by the Polish secret police. I reassured them on that point, and they went off with their microfilm to plot the overthrow of the Gomulka regime.

The Chinese garbage turned out to be almost entirely garbage, old interoffice memoranda and other such trivia. A friend of mine who teaches Far Eastern History at Columbia (the university, not the erstwhile dictatorship) went through the lot and translated enough for me to tell whether various documents were worth keeping. Most were not and went into the garbage can. But among the chaff there was one nice grain of wheat, a dossier of plans for the subversion of one of the little neutralist states in Africa. It had extensive analyses of various groups and factions in the government, names of Chinese agents, names of U.S. and Russian and French and British agents, and all sorts of vital bits of information and theory.

I had the feeling the Chinese had no real intention of putting the plan into effect, certainly not for the time being, with China too much in the grip of internal problems. The dossier had the tone of something drawn up by some bureaucrats who never expected to see it put into play. Still, it was worth more than consignment to the incinerator.

I thought of turning it over to the Chief, then changed my mind. The program was the sort of thing that anyone could put to use, and I rather like that little neutralist nation; I'd hate to see the Chinese overthrow it, but I wouldn't be much happier to see the CIA turn the same trick. And, after all, they do seem to have internal leaks.

I thought it over some more and wound up taking it to Washington and hiring a messenger to deliver it anonymously to the African nation's tiny embassy. Forewarned, I felt, was forearmed; now they would be better equipped to stave off attacks from Peking. Or, for that matter, from Washington.

A letter from Colombia (the country, not the college this time) was delivered to me by hand just the other morning. In careful language I was thanked at great length for my services and assured I would always be welcome. Should I care to come for a visit, I could expect the finest treatment.

If I can find the time, I'd like to go.

So that wraps it up, doesn't it? The Chinese documents, Milan and his book, Igor and his plane, Sofija and her gymnasts, Tadeusz and his microfilm, the passport, everything.

Oh, yes.

Minna.

When I got home from the Armenian meeting last night she was sitting in a chair reading *Alice in Wonderland*. She reads English almost as well as she speaks it, and she can get through almost anything now that I've taught her to use a dictionary. She would miss most of Lewis Carroll's puns, of course, but so do all children.

"Hi," she said. *"Cómo está?"*

*"Bien, gracias,"* I said. "Who's teaching you Spanish?"

"Paulie." Paulie, né Pablo, was the janitor's little boy. "And also Estrella." Estrella was the prostitute who lives on the second floor.

"Oh. Shouldn't you be asleep by now?"

"I will make you some coffee," she said. "And I will have a glass of milk."

She went into my little kitchen and made a cup of coffee for me. She brought it out along with a large glass of milk for herself. We sat together, and I sipped my coffee, and she drank her milk.

I said, "It was very nice of you to make the coffee, but it is still very late. Later than before you made the coffee. Don't you think you ought to go to sleep?"

"I will go to sleep when you go to sleep."

"I don't sleep. You know that."

"Sometimes you sleep, Evan."

"Never."

"When Zenta was living here——"

"That wasn't sleeping exactly." Zenta had spent a few days and nights with us, and it had not been sleeping, not at all. "That was different."

"I thought so."

"You don't miss a trick, do you?"

"Miss a trick?"

"You notice things, I mean."

"Some things I notice," she said.

"And on top of that you changed the subject. I don't go to sleep, you know that. But you have to sleep regularly or you'll be sick. You know that, too."

"Yes, Evan."

"So go put on your pajamas."

"Put them on what?"

"Put them on you." She was unsuccessfully repressing

a giggle. "You knew precisely what I meant. You knew *miss a trick,* too."

She quoted Humpty Dumpty: "'When I use a word, it means precisely what I wish it to mean, neither more nor less.'"

"Maybe I shouldn't let you read Alice. It's making you far too clever."

"I like it. Don't you like it, Evan?"

"Yes, very much. Go put on your pajamas. Now."

"Yes, Evan."

When she returned, properly pajama-clad, hands and face washed and teeth brushed, I asked her if she was ready to go to sleep now. She said that she was.

"We're going to have to find a home for you," I said.

"This is my home, Evan."

"A real home, I mean. You need a Mommy and a Daddy and——"

"Why? I like to live here. With you."

"A regular house," I said. "With a lawn out in front and a big back yard and grass and trees and flowers——"

"I love to go to Central Park," she said. "Grass and trees and flowers."

"And children to play with, and dogs and cats——"

"There are so many children here in this building for me to play with," she said. "Paulie and Rafael and Willie and Susan and so many others. And Eduardo lets me play with Ginger in the cellar, and Susan has a big dog named Baron, he is a German shepherd, but they speak to him in English. And there are all the animals in the zoo. I had a wonderful time when you took me to the zoo."

I went into the kitchen and made myself more coffee. I had the uncomfortable feeling that I wasn't getting my point across. I came back and couldn't find her. Then I went to the bedroom. She was sitting up in bed with the covers pulled up to her neck.

"You will have to start going to school," I said. "How will you learn anything?"

"But I learn so many things. English, Spanish, reading, writing, numbers, everything."

"Still, in a good school——"

"Paulie says school stinks. What does that mean?"

"That it smells bad. But——"

"I would not want to go to a place that smells bad."

"Well, what it means, really, is that Paulie doesn't like school, I suppose. But you would like it."

"Why?"

"Well——"

"I like it very much right here," she said. "I teach myself things out of your books, and other people teach me things, and you teach me the most of all, Evan. Why do I have to go to school so that I can learn things?"

"If you don't go to school, you can't go to college."

"What is college?"

"It's like school."

"Did you go to college?"

"No." This wasn't working out well at all. "There are laws," I said finally, "that say children must go to school. It is the law."

She looked at me.

"Well, it's the law."

"Will they put us in prison?"

"I don't think so."

"Besides, how will they find out? Who will tell them?"

"They might find out."

"Then, when they come to look for me, you will tell me, and I will quickly hide in the closet or under the bed."

"Minna——"

"And I will live here forever with Evan," she said. "And I will play with all my friends and I will learn many different languages and I will go to the zoo to see the animals and I will read all the books and study many things."

"Minna——"

"But now I must go to sleep," she said smoothly. "So that I will not become sick. And I will stay here forever, and when I am Queen of Lithuania, you will be my Prime Minister."

"Do you want to be Queen of Lithuania?"

"No. I want to live forever right here on 107th Street. May I stay here, Evan?"

"Well, for the time being."

"Forever?"

"We'll see how it works out."

She didn't say anything, and then her eyes slipped quietly shut, and she slept. I eased her down onto the bed, settled the pillow under her golden hair, tucked in the covers. When I bent over to kiss her good night she stirred.

"I will live here forever," she whispered. "Forever." And then she slid away to sleep again.

I turned out the light, left the room, closed the door. *I will live here forever, Evan.*

Well, why not? She's fun to have around.

# *Bestselling Books for Today's Reader*